T0157471

BLESSED ARE
THE HUNGRY

BLESSED ARE
THE HUNGRY

A Starving Artist,
A Depressed Businesswoman,
A Lonely Elderly Couple,
Who Needs Who?

JIM BORNZIN

BLESSED ARE THE HUNGRY
A STARVING ARTIST, A DEPRESSED BUSINESSWOMAN,
A LONELY ELDERLY COUPLE, WHO NEEDS WHO?

Copyright © 2020 Jim Bornzin.

All rights reserved. No part of this book may be used or reproduced by any means, graphic, electronic, or mechanical, including photocopying, recording, taping or by any information storage retrieval system without the written permission of the author except in the case of brief quotations embodied in critical articles and reviews.

iUniverse books may be ordered through booksellers or by contacting:

iUniverse
1663 Liberty Drive
Bloomington, IN 47403
www.iuniverse.com
1-800-Authors (1-800-288-4677)

Because of the dynamic nature of the Internet, any web addresses or links contained in this book may have changed since publication and may no longer be valid. The views expressed in this work are solely those of the author and do not necessarily reflect the views of the publisher, and the publisher hereby disclaims any responsibility for them.

Any people depicted in stock imagery provided by Getty Images are models, and such images are being used for illustrative purposes only.
Certain stock imagery © Getty Images.

ISBN: 978-1-5320-9520-7 (sc)
ISBN: 978-1-5320-9521-4 (e)

Library of Congress Control Number: 2020902898

Print information available on the last page.

iUniverse rev. date: 02/13/2020

CHAPTER ONE

A STARVING ARTIST

S top! Leave it alone! It'll never be perfect, so stop! He put down the brush and stepped back from the canvas. No, that tree needs a little more amber. He leaned forward to pick up the brush. No! Stop! Don't touch that brush! He turned away, but his eyes wanted to look again at his masterpiece. Don't look. Take a break. Promising himself he is finished, he walked to the refrigerator, opened the door, and was hit by the reality of his life. A month-old jar of pickles, a small package of moldy cheese, ketchup and mustard, two cans of beer and one cola. The milk was gone; he drank what was left in the carton yesterday. He sat down on the kitchen stool, folded his arms on the counter, laid his head on his arms, and tried to decide what to do next. But he couldn't do anything. He was just too depressed.

Hunter was glad to be done with college, though he hadn't graduated. He had moved into this rundown three-story apartment building on the near North Side of Chicago about six years ago. He heard himself exhaling through his nose and felt his chest expand and contract. He took a deep breath, raised his head and looked around the apartment. It was filled with his work. Finished canvases lined every wall, standing three deep in places. Acrylic was his favorite medium now. In high school he had fallen in love with oil painting. Now in his twenties, he found acrylics easier to clean up, and they dried faster. He gradually became aware of the traffic noise outside, then heard footsteps on the stairs. He glanced at the clock. 5:45 pm. That means Janet is coming home from work. He listened as she unlocked her apartment door and closed it behind her.

Janet had moved into the apartment building five years ago, just a year after he did. The first few times he saw Janet, his heart pounded pretty hard. She was beautiful. After a month or so, he saw past her make-up and eye-shadow and tight-fitting dresses. He guessed she was at least eight or ten years older than he. And judging by how she dressed, she must be making pretty good money. As they became acquainted, passing on the stairs or at the mailboxes, he learned she worked as a marketing manager for a large manufacturing firm. Maybe because he is so much younger, or probably because she has learned he is an artist and works at home, she has spoken only briefly to him. And when she does, he senses a touch of disdain in her voice.

There is an "art community" of sorts here on the near North Side. And the tuition money his parents had given him was enough to sign the lease, pay the first and last month's rent, and buy a new easel, several brushes, and some of the acrylic colors he needed.

A knock on his apartment door roused him from his thoughts. O shit! This place is a mess! I'm a mess! I can't believe she actually wants to talk to me. He walked nervously to the door, peered out the peephole, and saw the elderly woman who lives in the apartment between his and Janet's. What a relief! I'm glad it isn't her! He opened the door.

"Good afternoon, Mrs. Gerber, what can I do for you?"

"Hello Hunter. I just finished baking some fresh bread and rolls. Would you like some?"

"Well, certainly. Please come in."

"No, no. I don't want to bother you. Here's a bag with the goodies. You just enjoy them."

"Thank you so much! I can really use some fresh stuff right now."

"Still warm. Right out of the oven." She turned to leave.

"Is there anything I can do for you, Mrs. Gerber?"

"Someday . . . Mr. Gerber and I would love to have one of your paintings."

"Well, I'll have to give that some thought," Hunter answered.

Looking back over her shoulder, she replied with a grin, "Oh, never mind. I'm sure we could never afford one." Clara Gerber had been like a grandmother since he moved in. As she stepped away she gushed, "Your paintings are so beautiful!" The old woman opened her apartment door and disappeared inside.

Hunter put the bag on the kitchen counter and carefully lifted out a bag of warm dinner rolls and a loaf of freshly-baked wheat bread. The smell was heavenly. I'm glad she likes my paintings. But should I give them one? Or sell one to them? Full price or half price? God, I don't know what to do. Maybe they've got more money than I suspect. But I've never seen them splurge. Look at all these paintings! Just sitting here! I suppose I could give them one. He quickly spread butter on one of the rolls, opened his last Coke, and wolfed it down.

His thoughts shifted to his high school buddy, Nathan. The two of them talked about being artists someday. Nathan pursued his interest in college, majoring in Art History. For some reason, unknown to Hunter, Nathan quit drawing and painting. Instead, he opened an art gallery, and allowed Hunter to hang a few of his paintings for sale. Hunter worked part-time at a grocery store, sold a few paintings at Nathan's gallery, and was lucky his parents bailed him out now and then with rent money. He hated to beg, but without their help he'd be in a blanket on the street.

He glanced around the apartment again wondering what would become of all these canvases. Hunter got lost when he was painting. It would start with an idea, just a flash of an image, then a sketch.

And once he put the brush to canvas he was a goner. It was like entering an alternative universe. There was no passing of time, just an evolving image on the canvas. He loved the creative energy that flowed between his mind, his eyes, and his hands. He loved seeing the painting develop, come alive, and evolve. These were his children. He gave them birth. Sometimes painfully. Always excitedly. And now they lined his walls.

The really great ones were framed and hung on the wall. He simply couldn't part with those. The really good ones were framed and reluctantly turned over to Nathan for sale. And the good to average stood on the floor leaning against the walls. He had tried a few jobs after dropping out of college, but in his heart he knew he had only one love. He has to paint.

CHAPTER TWO

A DEPRESSED BUSINESSWOMAN

There's a knock on the door. She's exhausted. Janet had just changed from her work clothes into her sweat pants and shirt. She didn't want to talk to anybody. Who could that be? Probably someone from the apartment building, otherwise they'd be downstairs ringing the bell. Janet moved to the door, and through the peephole spied her elderly neighbor, Clara Gerber. She and her husband Bob lived next-door, between Janet's apartment and Hunter's. The Gerber's were probably in their late-seventies or early eighties, judging by their gray hair, outdated clothing, and friendly, but wrinkled faces. Janet opened the door.

"Mrs. Gerber, how are you?"

"Just fine, Janet. And how's yourself?"

"Just got home from work a few minutes ago. I'm beat."

"Maybe this'll give you a little energy. I just finished baking." She held up the bag.

"What could that be?"

"It's a loaf of wheat bread and some fresh dinner rolls. Mr. Gerber put them in the bag."

"How delightful! I just bought some strawberry jam. I'll put that on a dinner roll. Would you care to join me?"

"Thank you, dear, that's awfully sweet of you; but Mr. Gerber is waiting for me to fix dinner."

"It is so thoughtful of you to bring these baked goods. Thank you."

"We're just delighted to have you as a neighbor. Enjoy!" And with that, she was gone.

Janet pulled the jam from the refrigerator, spread it on the warm dinner roll, and savored it with delight. Clara Gerber had been doing this several times each year since Janet met them. She wished she knew more about Clara and Bob. They had brief conversations in passing, but Janet never had time to visit. The couple seemed lonely. She had never seen any visitors at the Gerber's apartment. Her thoughts returned to her job and her exhaustion.

Her media campaign had wrapped up on Thursday, and with any luck the orders would start pouring in online. She was proud of her work, happy with her salary, but running on empty. Jan's parents kept telling her to take care of herself. They don't understand the pressure. To succeed in marketing, you have to give your life to the company.

She's relieved to be out of the three year disastrous relationship with an alcoholic. She doesn't want to risk another. She doesn't see her parents or brother much anymore. She walked to the desk in her study, balanced her checkbook and responded to a few emails. She didn't feel like watching anything on TV, so she took a sleeping pill and crawled into bed. What am I doing? Why do I keep pushing myself? Why do I feel such a need to succeed?

For the next several nights she found herself repeating the pattern. Tonight, she fixed herself a frozen dinner, watched TV for an hour, turned it off, and sat there feeling depressed. Suddenly she heard a loud thump out in the hall. Someone screamed and then started yelling profanities. She recognized the voice of her neighbor, Hunter, so she got up and went to the door. Opening the door she couldn't help but laugh at what she saw. It was Hunter, leaning against the stairway railing holding his knee. He didn't appear to be seriously hurt. A bag of groceries littered the hall floor. A broken bottle of ketchup looked like a car wreck with lots of blood splattered across the tile.

"What happened to you?" she asked, trying to hide a smile.

"I tripped on the last stair and dropped my groceries, duuhh!" Hunter rolled up his pant leg and examined his badly bruised knee. Last thing he needed was Janet seeing him helpless.

Old Bob Gerber opened his door and looked out. "What's goin' on out here?" he hollered in a gruff voice.

"Poor Hunter fell and bumped his knee, and now he has an owwie," Janet giggled. She couldn't help making fun of the pathetic artist.

Bob stepped over the ketchup and reached out to pull Hunter off the floor.

His wife, Clara, appeared in the doorway and started barking orders. "Bob, you bring Hunter in here and fix up his knee. I'll pick up the mess on the floor. Janet, why don't you come over here and give me a hand cleaning this up."

Twenty minutes later Hunter finished his tale of woe. "I just don't know what I'm gonna do. I really can't work a 9-5 job, I just want to paint. But my paintings aren't selling enough to pay rent, let alone buy groceries. I have a few pieces in my friend's gallery, but there must be forty or fifty more in my apartment. Now I know why we're called starving artists."

Janet just wanted to tell him to "get a job," but realized it wasn't the proper thing to say at the moment.

"Here's what we're gonna do," Clara announced emphatically. "First, we happen to know Janet is very successful at her job in marketing. And you need help marketing your paintings. So Janet is going to work with you to help you sell your art."

"But I don't know anything about art," Janet interjected.

"Don't interrupt! Hunter will teach you about art, and you'll teach him about marketing."

"Yeah, but Janet has way more education than me," Hunter replied. "And I'm not sure we'd be able to work together."

"Hunter may have a point there," Janet added.

"You and Hunter don't have to like each other. You are simply being a good neighbor and helping him with your area of expertise. And Hunter, you don't want to be a 'starving artist' all your life, so you'd better be willing to work with Janet."

"Yeah, I suppose," he replied.

"Finally, I want both of you held accountable. So Bob and I will meet with you, all four of us, once a week, here in our apartment. Each of you can report on what you've done that week, and Bob and I can give you feedback and make suggestions." Clara looked each of them in the eye, waiting for their response.

"I guess I'm willing to give it a try," shrugged Hunter, reluctantly.

"I suppose I can too," replied Janet.

"We're all set then," Clara pronounced. "We'll see you back here in our apartment next Sunday night at seven p.m."

Janet and Hunter politely thanked Clara and Bob and made their way back to their respective apartments, not saying a word to each other. Neither could believe what they had just agreed to.

Back inside their apartment, Bob looked at his wife and shook his head. "Do you honestly think they can tolerate each other enough to work together?"

"Guess we'll just have to wait and see," Clara said with a smile.

CHAPTER THREE

MAN ON THE BENCH

H unter's knee still hurt and so did his ego. Janet laughing at him in the hall was not funny. And then she had the nerve to call my bruise "an owwie." I guess I didn't mind Bob putting the ice bag on my knee. And that Mrs. Gerber. I never knew she could be so bossy. Hunter put a few items, minus the ketchup, into the refrigerator. He thought about the painting he was working on but decided it was too late to start painting. He watched TV for an hour and went to bed.

For Hunter Sunday evening came much too soon. He remembered the discussion about meeting with the Gerbers and Janet. He wished he had never agreed to the crazy scheme Clara had suggested. Janet wasn't interested in his art. How could he teach her anything? On the other hand, maybe she could figure out a way to sell my paintings. Reluctantly he made his way to the Gerber's door and knocked.

Bob opened the door. "Hi Hunter. Come in. Janet just got here. She's in the kitchen helping Clara with some snacks." Bob and

Hunter took seats in the living room as Clara and Janet set snacks on the coffee table. Clara sat next to her husband and motioned for Janet to sit in the well-worn recliner. The flowered wallpaper looked like it had not been changed since the building was built in 1928.

Clara began the conversation, "Before we get started with our first official meeting, there's something we want to do. Bob and I have been discussing this since Hunter took his tumble on the stairs." She paused and turned to the artist. "Hunter, Bob and I want to buy one of your paintings."

Hunter was startled. "Which one?" he asked with a disbelieving frown.

Bob answered, "You know, that one with the guy asleep on the park bench and the pigeon on the back of the bench looking down at him?"

"The one with the sun coming through the trees," Clara added. "How much do you want for that one?"

"Oh, I don't know," Hunter sighed. "Maybe a couple hundred?"

"Well that's good," Bob replied, "because Clara and I have agreed we'd pay five hundred."

"Wow! Thanks. But that's more than..."

"I don't want to hear any arguing!" Clara interrupted. "Now you get back to your apartment and bring that one over here."

Hunter rose, unable to believe what was happening. Inside his apartment he looked at the painting of the guy on the park bench - - with the pigeon. He lifted it carefully off the wall. Darn, he kind of hated to part with this one. But they said they would pay $500, and that was more than anything he ever got paid before. He looked lovingly at the painting and kissed it good-by. He felt a little silly actually kissing the frame, but this was "one of his kids." He carried it into the hall and knocked again on the Gerber's door.

Bob opened the door. "Welcome back. I see you brought our favorite painting."

Hunter carefully handed his painting to Bob who held it, staring lovingly at this beloved work of art. Bob looked at Hunter and then at the painting. A man with scruffy gray hair and a beard was wrapped in a dirty plaid blanket and curled up on a park bench. His shabby boots stuck out from under the blanket and hung over the end of the bench. The morning sun shone through the trees highlighting the pigeon perched just above his head.

"Thank you, Hunter. Clara and I will treasure this forever. I think we'll hang it in our bedroom. It will remind me and Clara to be thankful every night for our warm, safe, comfortable bed." Bob handed it carefully back to Hunter. "Here, you give it to Clara. I'll go get your check."

Clara and Janet came out from the kitchen. Hunter held out the painting.

"Oh, Hunter, I just love it!" Clara gushed. She took the painting from Hunter and showed it to Janet.

"I can see why you like it," Janet said admiringly. "I've heard people say that good art touches the soul. This one makes me sad because of the old man, but the pigeon brings a smile to my face. It's like he's telling the old man everything's going to be okay."

"Thanks," was all Hunter could say. He knew his work had found a good home.

In a few moments Bob was back in the room. He handed Hunter a check for $500.

Trying to pretend it was no big deal, Hunter tucked the check into his billfold. "Thanks."

"Okay, everyone, it's time for our meeting," Clara announced.

CHAPTER FOUR

THE FIRST OFFICIAL MEETING

C lara invited them to help themselves to the snacks she had placed on the coffee table. "Bob's had more business experience than I, so Bob, why don't you call this meeting to order?"

"All right. Let's begin. Maybe it would be a good idea, since we don't know a lot about each other, for us to get better acquainted. Take five or ten minutes to introduce yourself. Tell us where you were born, where you went to school, and anything else you're willing to share. Hunter, why don't you begin?"

Hunter shrugged, "I don't know what to tell you. I was born in Arlington Heights where my parents still live. My dad's an auto mechanic. He's worked in the same shop as long as I can remember. Mom never worked. At least not that I know about. I don't think either one went to college, so they really wanted me to. Go to college, I mean."

Janet commented, "Last week you told us you dropped out because you wanted to paint."

"Yeah, that's all I really wanted to do.

"Where do you show them?" she asked.

"That's the problem," he replied. "My friend Nathan has a few at his gallery. In fact he's even sold a couple."

"And what's your hope for the future?" Bob asked.

Hunter shrugged. "I don't know. I guess I'd just like to sell more paintings." Everyone nodded. No one spoke.

"Okay, Janet, I guess it's your turn," Bob said.

"Well, I was born in Atlanta, Georgia."

"But you don't have a southern accent," Hunter observed.

"That's because we moved to Kansas City, then Bismark, then Milwaukee."

"That's a lot of moving, young lady," Bob commented.

"My dad was a resort hotel manager. He really knows how to work with people. Builds a team that respects and trusts him. He always called them 'his team' never 'his staff.' He's a good manager and businessman. But once he gets things running smoothly, he's ready for a new challenge. I guess that's why we moved so often."

"And where did you go to college, dear?" Clara asked.

"University of Wisconsin. Two years at Milwaukee then I transferred to Madison and graduated from there with an M.B.A."

"Very impressive," Bob replied.

"My parents are still in Milwaukee, but my older brother is married and living in California. He and his wife have two children, but we don't get to see them very often."

"What happened after you graduated?" Bob asked.

"I worked for a short time in Milwaukee for a clothing company, then I came down here to Chicago with my present job."

"What exactly do you do now?" Clara inquired.

"I'm the Online Marketing Manager for ApplianceCo. We manufacture all kinds of home appliances. I'm in charge of all the online promotion of our products here in the Midwest division."

"You lived in Milwaukee. You a beer drinker?" Hunter asked.

"Not really. I prefer wine, but I don't drink much."

"I'm a Pabst Blue Ribbon man, myself," Hunter added.

"I had a partner for about three years, but he drank too much. Guess that's why I'm not married," Janet continued. "I wouldn't mind, some day, but I'm okay by myself."

"It's better not to rush into marriage," Clara replied.

"And how about you two?" Janet asked Clara. "How long have you been married?"

Bob and Clara looked at each other and smiled. "Almost fifty years," Clara answered.

"We met here in Chicago," Bob began. "I graduated from IIT, the Illinois Institute of Technology and was working for Illinois Bell Telephone Company. We were setting up a phone system in the offices where Clara worked."

Clara picked up the story. "He was crawling around underneath desks, connecting wires, and telephones. I thought he was cute, so I teased him, 'Is this how you check out women?' I asked. 'Crawling around on the floor so you can peek up their skirt?' He turned beet red."

"I did not," Bob replied gruffly. "I remember distinctly what I said. I said, 'This is my job and crawling on my knees keeps me humble. I'd get on my knees for you any day.'"

Everyone chuckled. "Then, from my kneeling position, I asked if she'd go out to dinner with me, and she accepted."

"Six months later he was on his knees again," Clara interrupted, "and this time he proposed."

"We've had a good marriage, and I had a good career with the phone company," Bob went on. "The only disappointment for both of us is we never had any children."

"It gets kind of lonely around here. Especially on the holidays," Clara added.

"Clara has her knitting and goes to the Senior Center for some of their activities. I mostly like to read, especially science fiction."

"Bob and I have done some traveling since we retired. We went to Europe on a two week tour about five years ago. The history of those cities and cathedrals and castles was amazing, but we got so tired of traveling from place to place, we just wanted to get home. And we've been pretty much home bodies ever since." Clara looked at Bob and smiled.

"Yeah, we're just thankful to have each other," Bob nodded.

"Help yourselves to some more cookies," Clara motioned toward the plate.

Hunter and Janet each picked up another cookie and sipped their lukewarm coffee. Bob rapped his knuckles on the coffee table. "Okay, now it's time to get down to business. Clara and I have had several discussions the past few days. She has some ideas about what needs to be done."

"Well, as Bob said, we've talked a lot about the two of you. And as I said before, you don't even have to like each other, but we feel you can both learn something from each other. Hunter and Janet, I want both of you to get in a business frame of mind. The first thing you'll need to do is carefully review Hunter's paintings. Look at them very carefully. Hunter, I want you to do your best to explain your art to Janet. Do you think you can do that?"

"Yeah, I'll give it a shot. I hope she'll understand why I get excited about painting."

"Janet, during the next few days, you will visit several art galleries here in the city, and talk with the managers. Learn as much as you can about how they obtain their inventory. What kind of contract does the artist sign? What kind of prices are being charged? And what percentage goes to the gallery and how much to the artist? Take notes if you need to. Is that clear?"

"Yeah, I think so," Janet replied reluctantly.

"Your job is to get his paintings on the market. Maybe you can help him set up a website with photos of his paintings. Get as many as you can into the local galleries."

"And Hunter," Clara continued, "your job is to spend at least one day a week on marketing and sales of your paintings. One day a week. Got that?"

"I thought you said Janet was going to do the marketing."

"One day a week you go with Janet, learning how to market your work. I know you won't like doing it. However . . . spending one day doing something you don't like to do will make you appreciate the next day at your easel even more. Is that clear?"

"I guess," Hunter said with a frown.

"Well, let's not waste any time," Clara continued. "I think you both have your assignments. Bob and I are here to give you both a swift kick in the pants. Hunter, take Janet to your apartment right now and show her your paintings."

"My apartment's a mess. I don't want her coming over tonight," Hunter complained.

"Nonsense. If you don't do it tonight, you'll just put it off indefinitely. Now get going."

"Meeting adjourned," Bob added.

They all rose, glancing at each other. As Clara and Bob walked them toward the door, Janet thanked them politely. Hunter smiled and nodded, but he was mad and disgusted. This wasn't what he had expected. He really didn't want Janet in his apartment.

CHAPTER FIVE

THE PARTNERSHIP BEGINS

H unter unlocked the door, turned on the lights, and invited her in.

"Sorry about the mess," he offered.

"No problem." Janet forced a smile. "Let's see those paintings."

They spent half an hour looking through the many canvases strewn around the apartment.

"This is one of my favorites," Hunter said proudly as he propped the canvas onto the easel. "I haven't done many snow scenes, but this one makes me cold just looking at it."

"Yeah, I like it," Janet replied. "How much are you asking for it?"

"Oh, I don't know. I'm thinking maybe five or six hundred. It took me nearly a week."

"Well, like I said, I don't know anything about art; but I do like it."

"Thanks," Hunter said, blushing slightly.

"I noticed all your paintings are signed 'Hunter.' But there's a different name on your mailbox downstairs. Is Hunter your last name, or your given name?"

He laughed. "My full name is Hunter Schlewitz. As an aspiring artist I decided I would rather sign Hunter on paintings. Schlewitz just seemed too awkward for people to remember, and it's hard to spell."

Janet laughed. "Don't ask ME to spell it."

"Well, I think you've seen everything," Hunter said as he looked around the room.

"Not quite," Janet replied. "What's that?" She pointed at a basket with knitting needles, several skeins of yarn, and a half-finished shawl.

"Aw... Geez! I forgot that was out. I wasn't expecting any visitors."

"Looks like someone knits," Janet couldn't help but grin.

"I suppose I could tell a little lie and say it belongs to my mom and she left it here."

"Yeah, but we both know that's not the truth."

"Okay, so I like to knit when I'm not painting . . . It kinda helps me step away from the easel and take a break. It gets my mind off the painting. But please, don't tell anybody."

"Oh, my lips are sealed. The Gerbers will never hear it from me." Janet smiled.

Hunter was embarrassed and wanted desperately to change the subject. "So what do we do now?" he asked. "I don't know a damn thing about marketing."

"For starters, why don't you make a list of all your paintings? Do you have a laptop?"

"Yeah, but I don't type very well."

"That doesn't matter. Just give each of your paintings a name, and estimate a price you'd like to receive for it. I'll start visiting galleries just to get a feel for this whole thing. I needed something to do after work. It might even be good for me."

"Gee, I don't know what good this is gonna do, but thanks for tryin'."

"I might even learn something about art!" Janet took a step toward the door.

"Thanks for comin' over," Hunter replied as she stepped into the hall.

"G'night," she smiled.

"G'night. Talk to you tomorrow." Hunter watched her walk toward her apartment and slowly shut his door. Darn it! Never should have left my knitting basket on the ledge. He took a deep breath, pulled the $500 check from his pocket and set it on the counter. He was glad tonight was over. Tomorrow, he'd pay his overdue rent.

CHAPTER SIX

A LONELY ELDERLY COUPLE

B ob and Clara were excited to rehash the meeting after Hunter and Janet left. Clara cleared the snacks to the kitchen and came back into the living room holding a dish towel. Bob had picked up the newspaper and had his face buried in the sports page. Clara snapped the towel toward the newspaper making a loud POP! Bob nearly jumped out of the chair.

"I haven't had that much fun in years!" Clara giggled.

"I thought you were in the kitchen," Bob replied. "You scared the heck out of me. And to tell the truth, I didn't find *that* fun at all."

"I was talking about the Hunter's art meeting, silly."

"I thought you meant popping me with the towel."

"No, the meeting. Wasn't that fun with Janet and Hunter?"

"Yeah, I think it went pretty well," Bob answered.

"I thought you did a really nice job conducting the meeting."

"Thanks, honey. That was kind of fun."

"I like how you started with the get-acquainted talks. I didn't know Janet had lived in so many cities in her young life."

"That was interesting," Bob agreed. "But I'm glad we never had to move that much."

"Only three times since we've been married, and all three of our homes have been right here in Chicago. Remember our first apartment on Kedzie?"

"I sure do. We could hardly move without bumping into each other." Bob smiled.

Clara sat down next to him in her favorite chair. "But remember how fun it was to bump into each other when we were first married?" Clara tilted her head and grinned.

"How could I forget?" Bob grinned back. "But you were glad when we moved into our first house, remember? Two bedrooms, and a full basement. I loved my workshop down there."

"We thought surely I'd get pregnant with the extra room for the baby."

"Yeah, but it didn't happen," Bob looked sorrowfully into Clara's eyes, a look she understood as apology.

"True, but you had your workshop and I had my garden." Clara spoke lovingly.

"I know you wanted children," Bob continued.

"True, but we had each other," Clara reassured him. "And your career with Illinois Bell provided well, when you were working, and now in retirement."

"When I retired we decided to down-size by selling the house. Do you still feel okay about moving into another apartment when I retired?" Bob asked.

"Absolutely. We both agreed the house was requiring too much maintenance." Clara smiled knowingly. "And to think, we've been here nearly twenty years!"

"And the interest we're earning from our equity is paying our rent," Bob added.

"My husband, the business whiz," Clara smiled again. She pretended she was going to pop him again with her towel.

Bob held up his hands defensively. "Speaking of business whiz," he said, "that Janet seems like a really sharp young woman."

"I agree," Clara answered. "I certainly hope she can teach Hunter a thing or two."

"You know," Bob replied, "I think Hunter is desperate enough to want to learn."

"But the question is this: Is he desperate enough to work with Janet?" Both Clara and Bob burst out laughing.

"As you said, Time will tell." Bob shrugged his shoulders and grinned. "I'm glad you suggested we meet with them once a week to keep things on track."

Clara rose and headed back to the kitchen. "I just love what we're doing. It's almost like having a couple of grown kids we still feel responsible for."

"Just don't get carried away with this project of yours," Bob said with exaggerated wisdom.

"Oh Bob, aren't you having fun too?"

"Well, I've got to admit, I did enjoy conducting that meeting of ours."

Clara washed up the dishes and Bob finished reading the sports page. As they headed into the bedroom, Clara bumped him, pushing him into the door. "What are you doing?" Bob asked, puzzled.

"Just pushing you around, old man," she teased.

"You really are getting pushy in your old age," he teased in return.

"In my old age? Heck, I've been pushy since the day we met," Clara bragged.

"And that's why I married you," Bob replied smartly. "I needed someone to keep me in line."

They got into their pajamas and crawled under the covers. "I just remembered," Clara said, "I promised Penny I'd help serve lunch at the Senior Center tomorrow. So I'll have to leave about 11 o'clock."

"It's good for you to get out of the apartment once in a while," Bob commented.

"YOU should get out more often. Want to join us for lunch at the Center?" Clara invited him.

"What? Sit and talk with all those OLD people?" Bob teased. "No thanks."

"Listen, buster, you keep sitting around this apartment by yourself and everyone will call YOU a Lonely Old Man." Clara wished Bob was more sociable but knew he never would be.

"As long as I've got you, sweetheart, I'll NEVER be a lonely old man." Bob reached out and caressed her cheek.

Clara stretched forward and gave him a good-night kiss. "Love you. Sleep tight."

"Love you too. Pleasant dreams." Bob turned over and silently prayed his thankfulness. Both of them were asleep in minutes.

CHAPTER SEVEN

MARKETING BEGINS

J anet made it a point to arrive at work early. The social media campaign had really taken off. Nearly five hundred comments in the first day! The vice-president of marketing complimented her in front of the entire staff. When she returned to her desk she saw the list of art galleries she had researched at home last night. She was excited to visit the galleries to learn more about art exhibits. She glanced at the clock. 5:30 pm couldn't come soon enough.

That afternoon Janet left work with a destination in mind. At the first gallery on her list, a young woman welcomed her and talked about the artists whose work was being shown. Janet walked through the gallery, observing mostly flowers and fairies, impressionist and abstract art.

"We feature local women artists whose work is truly inspirational," the hostess gushed. Janet realized this was not the place for Hunter's work, but decided to push for more information. "Do your artists have a contract for displaying their work here?"

"Yes, would you like to see a copy?"

"Thank you, do you mind if I take this home?"

"Not at all. Do you have some work you'd like to show here?"

"I'm exploring possibilities. Is this the usual percentage for the gallery?"

"Yes, as you can see, we've penciled in 30-50%. Some galleries ask 60%."

Janet thanked the attendant and left with the contract in her purse.

After one more gallery visit, she was hungry, picked up an order to go, and hopped on the bus for a short ride back to the apartment. She ate a quick supper with one eye on the TV news report. She rinsed the dishes and headed for Hunter's door.

"Hi, Janet. C'mon in," Hunter opened the door and stepped back.

Janet walked in and glanced around the apartment. Hmm, somewhat tidier than my previous visit. And no knitting basket in sight. "I had a couple of interesting gallery tours this afternoon."

"Where did you go?" Hunter asked.

"The first was strictly women's art. I don't think your paintings would fit in there."

"What do you mean, women's art. Art is art."

"Oh, it was all flowers and birds and butterflies and fairies, and definitely not your style. But the second gallery had quite a variety. Oils, watercolor, ceramics, sculptures, a little of everything."

"How much would they gouge me for?" Hunter asked.

"Calm down. I get the feeling that all the galleries want somewhere between 30% and 50% of the sale price."

"Geez that seems high. Just for some wall space and lighting."

"Remember, they have to pay rent, heating and electric bills, a salesperson on duty. It's a business like any other."

"Yeah, right."

"Did you finish your inventory of paintings and your asking prices?"

"Just about. I'm really not sure how to price them." He handed Janet the sheet.

She placed it on the kitchen counter and started writing new prices next to Hunter's.

"Whoa! What are you doing?" Hunter said as he looked over her shoulder.

"Adding about a third to all your figures."

"I'm not sure they'll sell for that much."

"Oh, of course they will. And now you don't have to worry about how much the gallery is taking. You'll get what you wanted in the first place."

Hunter frowned. "Hmm. Maybe you've got a point. But now I'll have to re-type the whole list. Or at least the prices."

Janet finished her scribbling and looked up at him. "And how long did it take you to make this list?"

"Three or four hours, I think." Hunter said, wondering why she needed to know. He was embarrassed it had taken him so long.

"Okay, about half a day's work. So, here's what I was thinking. Tomorrow, when I'm done at the office, you meet me at one of the galleries, and we'll do a little exploring together."

"No, I don't think so. I'm the painter. You do the marketing, remember?"

"One day a week, you learn to do marketing. Remember what Mrs. Gerber said?"

"Aw, geez. Why did you have to bring that up?" Hunter frowned.

"Look, buster, I'm not enjoying this any more than you are!"

"All right, all right. Where should we meet?"

"Why don't you come to the lobby of my firm and I'll take it from there."

"What time?"

"Five thirty. And don't wear those filthy jeans," she pointed at his legs.

Hunter grinned. "What's wrong with a little paint splatter? At least people will know I'm an artist."

"Or just a sloppy painter!" Janet frowned and made her way to the door. As she let herself out she looked back. "Don't wear those!"

Hunter hated this whole thing. He wasn't sure why he had

agreed to it in the first place. He didn't like Janet telling him what to do. He didn't like Janet, period. He didn't need another mother. He didn't need a business partner. He opened the refrigerator to get a beer. One left. Then he remembered. Oh yeah, I need to make some money or I won't be able to buy another beer. Or pay my rent. Or do anything else for that matter. He popped open the beer, sat down on the kitchen stool, folded his arms on the counter, and laid his head on his arms.

Janet, on the other hand, wasn't nearly as depressed as she had been a week ago. She could hardly stand the lazy, good-for-nothing artist with the crappy attitudes. But she was learning a little about art, and what she had learned so far, made her grateful to have a well-paying job in business. She considered buying a set of watercolors and a few brushes just to give art a try. Of course, if she did, she wouldn't tell Hunter.

CHAPTER EIGHT

THE SECOND MEETING

B ob and Clara Gerber were excited about hosting the second
meeting of the "Hunter Art Corporation" Board of Directors.
It had been a little over a week since Hunter's fateful fall on the
stairs. Janet showed up on time and a few minutes later Hunter
knocked on their door. Bob invited them to take seats in the living
room while Clara poured hot tea to go with her freshly baked
cookies.

"Mmm, these are delicious," beamed Janet.

"Yeah, they're really good," added Hunter.

"Well, if there are any left at the end of the meeting, I thought
the 'starving artist' could take home the left overs." Clara smiled
at Hunter.

"In that case, you're all welcome to eat one or two," Hunter
replied, chuckling.

"Well, I'm anxious to hear how the week went for both of you,"
Bob added. "Hunter, why don't you start with your report?"

"I had a pretty good week. Finished one acrylic and started a second."

"And did you do your one day of marketing?" Bob asked.

"Yeah," Hunter glanced at Janet, "but I can't say I enjoyed it."

"Tell 'em what we did," Janet chimed in.

"First thing Janet made me do was an inventory of all my paintings, with size and prices. Then I had to go with her and visit galleries."

"How many galleries did you visit?" Clara asked.

"Two."

"He came with me to two, but I went to eight in all," Janet interjected.

"And what did you learn from your visits?" Bob asked Hunter.

"Not much," he replied.

"Is that all you've got to say, Hunter? Not much?" Clara asked. Hunter shrugged.

"And what did you learn, Janet?" Bob asked.

"Quite a bit, actually. The main thing was getting a feel for the art world. I've never been involved before, other than walking through an art museum when I was in New York. Every gallery is different, depending on the owner or manager. The style of art, the way it is displayed, the commission amount, the wording of contracts, the way artists are invited or involved."

"Are you satisfied with your first week?" Clara asked.

"Oh, definitely. But I've got so much more to do in terms of relationship building. If I plan to represent Hunter's art, I'll have learn more about how to 'pitch' his work. And I'll have to decide which galleries would be most suitable for showing it."

"And that is exactly why I can't stand marketing," Hunter interjected. "Meeting people and talking, meeting and talking. No thanks."

Clara rose from the sofa, "Hunter! You stop that right now!" She stood looking down at the young artist. "We all know you love to paint. And we believe your art is good. But if you're ever going to sell any of it, you'll have to put forth some effort."

"And maybe show a little gratitude," Bob added.

There was a long pause in the conversation. Hunter squirmed uncomfortably. "I guess you're right. So what am I supposed to do this week?"

"Will you come with me to visit a few more galleries?" Janet asked.

"Yeah, I guess."

CHAPTER NINE

GET 'EM FRAMED

The following week went pretty smoothly. Janet decided which galleries most fit the needs of her client. She had tried thinking of him as a friend, but decided "client" better fit their relationship. She made copious notes on each gallery, including the names of managers, pluses and minuses in her opinion. Hunter's opinions were also noted. They visited three galleries together, and she visited four more without Hunter. She made separate files for each gallery in her PC, and the data was growing rapidly. She and Hunter finally decided to pitch his work to five or six galleries, hoping at least four would accept. Her calendar was filling with appointments and possible show dates. Janet urged Hunter to get as many of his paintings framed as he possibly could.

Hunter agreed to explore art and craft stores for the nicest, and most economical frames. The trouble was, he was broke. How could he buy frames? He was reluctant to call his parents, but where else could he get his hands on some cash? At least he had a plan and was moving forward with Janet and her ideas for marketing.

Building up his courage, Hunter finally made the phone call. His dad sounded cautious on the phone, but his mom argued in favor of giving him $300. His dad demanded he send a copy of the receipts to them, and Hunter agreed to do it. He hated being treated like a teenager, but he didn't want to argue.

When Hunter told Bob and Clara that he was going shopping for frames, they suggested he check out the ads for rummage sales, the Salvation Army, and Goodwill stores. The next day he started by visiting a couple of church rummage sales and ended his shopping at Goodwill. He returned to the apartment excited to show his purchases to the Gerbers. Balancing two arms full of purchases, he stumbled on the stairs, nearly dropping the frames. He knocked at the Gerber's door to show them.

"You were right, Clara! The sales were amazing. Look what I got for $85. Aren't these great? Most of them were only $5, and some were $8 or $10. There's twelve frames here. Some are in pretty rough condition, but that makes the painting look old and valuable." Hunter's enthusiasm was contagious as he showed Bob and Clara his treasured frames.

"Tell you what," said Bob, "Clara and I would like to buy these for you. Let me get my checkbook."

"No, no. My parents already gave me some money for frames," Hunter argued.

"You'll need more than twelve," Clara replied. "Bob, go get your checkbook."

Within minutes Bob handed Hunter another check, this one for $100.

"Wow! Wow! How can I ever thank you?"

"By getting those paintings framed and into a gallery," Clara responded.

"Ooo, that reminds me. Tomorrow I'm meeting with Janet, and we're taking several of my pieces to the Maple Street Gallery, to see if they'll do a show and display. Janet's been explaining how we'll discuss the contract before signing anything. She even said she'd negotiate for a better percentage for me."

"It sounds like you and Janet are learning how to work together," Clara replied.

"I don't see as how I've got much choice. At least with her I see the possibility of getting my work out in public, and I guess that's the only way it'll ever sell."

"Smart man," Bob replied. "You'll get the hang of it yet!"

The three of them shared a hearty laugh. Hunter picked up his twelve frames, anxious to get into his apartment and start framing his paintings.

Clara and Bob couldn't wait to tell Janet about the embers of excitement beginning to glow in Hunter.

CHAPTER TEN

HUNTER'S FIRST SHOWING

66 **I** 'll just take three or four of my paintings to each gallery. I'm sure they'll take just a few at a time. That way I'll get the most exposure all around town."

"Absolutely not!" Janet argued. "They'll get lost in the midst of other artists' work."

"Well, nobody's gonna take thirty all at once from an unknown artist!"

"Then we'll have to make you 'known.' What about your friend, Nathan? Would he be willing to consider a show of your work?"

"How would I know?" Hunter was frustrated with Janet's pushiness.

"You could ask him." Janet's glare was more than Hunter could bear.

"Why don't YOU ask him? You're supposed to be my agent, right?" Hunter got off the kitchen stool and walked into the living room.

"But he's YOUR friend, not mine," Janet replied stubbornly.

Hunter walked to a nearby easel, picked up a brush, and pretended to begin painting. A long silence followed as both wondered why things always turned sour.

"Here's what I think might work," Janet finally continued. "Why don't we both have a visit with your friend Nathan? We could bring several of your best pieces from here. Then ask him if he would consider a show featuring your work?"

"I told you, I don't want to sell the ones on the wall!" Hunter interrupted.

"Well, we could mark them 'Not for Sale.' But you have to admit, they'd get people's attention."

"Yeah. I guess. Let me think about it."

The more Hunter thought about it, the more he had to admit, Janet had some good ideas. The following week Hunter and Janet went to Nathan to present their proposal for a showing of Hunter's paintings. Nathan discussed the in's and out's of gallery business. He agreed to a one month show in September featuring Hunter's work, a total of forty paintings. Among those on display will be ten of Hunter's favorites, marked NFS.

Nathan had no complaint about the asking prices on the other works. The higher the price, the bigger his cut. He and Janet discussed advertising for the show, and she agreed to finance ads in the local art newsletter. Nathan also agreed to feature the show on his website and social media posts. Although Hunter wanted to be home alone painting, Janet insisted he meet with her and Nathan to approve what they were doing. Secretly, Janet kept hoping the dumb artist would learn something about marketing.

When they gathered at the Gerber's apartment for their weekly meeting, Janet was excited to share information about the show. She told the Gerbers, "This will give Hunter's work some traction, and make it easier to get shows at the other galleries in town. I think our artist's career is about to take off."

"That sounds wonderful, Janet. And Hunter, how are you feeling about all this?" Clara asked.

"Pretty good, I guess."

"You guess??!!" Clara nearly hollered. "Where's your excitement? Where's your enthusiasm? You're about to become a famous artist!"

"Oh, I wouldn't go that far. I'll be happy if I sell a few of the paintings."

Bob joined the conversation, "Hunter, my boy, you're still a young man. But you need to have more confidence in yourself. If you don't want to take credit for your talent, give God the glory. You can be humble, and still take pride in your art."

"My parents always told me I could never make a living being an artist. I guess I believed them. But I never wanted to do anything else."

Janet chimed in, "Hunter, you and I don't get along sometimes. But it's because we're just so different. Not because there's anything wrong with you."

Hunter had no reply, but he was trying to believe what she had just said, "not anything wrong with me." The words kept repeating in his mind.

"When is the opening for the show?" Clara asked.

"First of September, the Friday before Labor Day," Janet replied. "Nathan and I agree Hunter should be there for the opening weekend. Visitors to the gallery will want to meet the artist." Janet and the Gerbers looked at Hunter, waiting for his reply.

Hunter shrugged his shoulders. "I'm an artist, not a salesman."

"Hunter?" Bob was tired of Hunter's excuses.

"Yeah, yeah, I'll be there. All weekend."

The opening Friday night, Hunter was there in clean jeans, white shirt, and loose-fitting tie. He couldn't be more uncomfortable, and he was just a little scared. Janet showed up in a business suit. Nathan took Hunter aside to give him some words of encouragement.

"Relax, buddy. It's gonna go just fine. I've had a good response from social media. A lot of my regular patrons are excited to see your work."

"Thanks, Nathan. I really owe you big time."

"Don't thank me. Thank Janet. It wouldn't have happened without her."

Throughout the evening, people approached Hunter expressing admiration for his artwork. He appreciated their gushing and fawning, but doubted anyone would buy anything. The prices were probably too high. Janet enjoyed mingling with patrons, pretending to know more about art than she did, and speaking highly about her (client, ooops) friend Hunter.

At nine o'clock the last of the browsers walked out the door, leaving Hunter, Janet, and Nathan alone in the gallery. Hunter wanted nothing more than to get out of there. Janet was curious and asked Nathan, "Were there any sales tonight?"

Nathan looked at Hunter, "You really want to know?"

"Of course," Janet replied.

"I guess," Nathan sighed.

"Four sales on opening night! I think that ties the record!"

"Really!!" Janet jumped up and down, and reached out to give Nathan a hug.

Hunter was glad Janet didn't try to hug him. "Which ones?" Hunter asked.

"Does it really matter?" Janet replied. "Aren't you thrilled? We sold four of your paintings!"

"And tied an opening night record. At least since I've owned the gallery," Nathan added.

"Yeah, you're right. I guess it doesn't matter which ones."

"Not only that, but several people expressed interest in buying but said they wanted to give it some thought. That means they may be back tomorrow or Sunday."

"Congratulations, Hunter," Janet looked him in the eye. "A successful opening night." She put her arms out and Hunter opened his arms, reluctantly allowing her to hug him.

CHAPTER ELEVEN

GOOD REPORT – BAD REPORT

T hey all called it the Board of Directors meeting and laughed about the small size of their informal corporation. And they continued meeting weekly. They decided Sunday evening worked best, but from now on they would meet on the first and third Sunday of each month. Bob Gerber became the president, though a vote was never officially taken.

The show at Nathan's gallery yielded seven paintings sold, all for the price Hunter had specified. For the first time in his life, Hunter began to believe he might be able to make a living as an artist. The popularity of his work made it easier to convince other galleries to sponsor shows as well. Brightside Gallery agreed to display his work in October. Hunter and Janet were still working on November. Janet told the Board of Directors the real coup was December. The largest gallery in town, the Maple Street Gallery, signed Hunter Schlewitz for the month before Christmas. Holiday gift shopping would be at its peak.

Janet was able to back off just a little. Hunter seemed to be managing well, once the contracts were signed. He worked with gallery managers to determine what would be shown, and was prompt getting it to the gallery for set-up. He enjoyed choosing which works would be featured and where they'd be hung. Janet's company ramped up for the holidays and expected her to put in extra hours on social media promotions and ad campaigns.

The second Sunday in December was the 12th this year. Clara welcomed Hunter and Janet into their apartment, poured coffee, and passed the Christmas cookies she had baked. Bob called the meeting to order. Hunter proudly reported eight paintings sold, including three new ones he had done specifically for the Maple Street show.

"Congratulations, Hunter!" Janet was proud of his sales, and proud to be part of getting him motivated.

"I was wondering," Hunter asked, "have you lined up anything for January or February?"

"Not yet. I've been swamped at work," Janet replied. "ENVISION Gallery is the next one I had in mind. Maybe you and I could meet with them before Christmas. They may have artists lined up for the next several months, so we'd better hustle."

"You're right. I'll call for an appointment," said Hunter, "and ask what months might be available."

"That would be a good idea. And let me know what you find out. I'll make time after work if you get a time to meet with them," Janet reassured him.

During a brief pause in the discussion, Clara asked Bob if she might present their concern to Janet and Hunter. "Sure," he replied. "Now would probably be a good time."

"Dear friends, Bob and I have some sad news to share with you. This past week we saw our primary care doctor to get the reports on Bob's x-rays and tests. About ten years ago, Bob went through treatment for prostate cancer. Chemo and radiation were effective in destroying the cancer at that time, but now it has returned. Not only that . . . it has spread."

Janet looked from Clara to Bob. "I'm so sorry to hear that. How bad is it? Is there anything they can do?"

Bob shook his head.

Clara answered, "The doctor suggested aggressive treatment beginning with chemo, then radiation and more chemo."

"I don't want it," Bob added forcefully. "No chemo, no nothing."

"I think you should do it," Hunter suggested. "Sounds like it's your only chance."

"Have you ever had chemo?" Bob asked him.

"No. But I . . I don't want to think about the alternative."

"Well I have," Bob replied strongly. "I've thought about dying and I'm not afraid to say the word. And I've thought about chemo and radiation; and at my age, dying sounds better."

"Isn't there anything else they can do?" Janet asked.

"Well, of course, there's hospice and pain meds to keep me comfortable."

"Yes, but that won't be for a while," Clara added.

"How much time do you think you'll have without treatments?" Hunter asked.

"The doctor said it was hard to predict," Bob answered, "anywhere from a month to maybe six months."

"Oh, Clara, dear Bob, I'm so sad for you," Janet stood and stepped toward Bob. She bent over and gave him a hug. Then she turned to Clara who rose from her chair, and they embraced.

The rest of the evening passed with small talk about the weather. Bob and Clara both commended Hunter on his shows and sales. Hunter was looking forward to Hanukkah and wrapping up the year with a celebration of his earnings. Now he realized it would also be a sad holiday. Bob and Clara have become like parents to him, and he couldn't imagine his life without Bob.

CHAPTER TWELVE

HANUKKAH AND CHRISTMAS DAY

Before Hunter and Janet left the Gerber's apartment, Clara invited them to come over on Christmas day for coffee and cookies.

Janet smiled and shook her head, "I promised my folks I'd drop by at their house that afternoon. Why don't you all plan to come to my apartment that evening? I'll have the coffee and snacks prepared."

"That would be so kind of you, my dear," Clara responded.

"What time?" Hunter asked.

"Seven?" Janet suggested.

"Sounds good to me," Hunter answered.

"We'll be there," Clara added. "And I'll bring some cookies to add to the fun."

As they left Hunter shook Bob's hand, looked into his eyes, and wished he knew what to say. He simply turned away. Janet gave Bob a hug and whispered, "See you Christmas Day."

Clara promised to keep them posted on Bob's condition. "We'll plan to meet the first Sunday in January, if Bob is feeling okay."

Hunter and Janet made their way to the door.

On the first day of Hanukkah Hunter drove to Arlington Heights to be with his parents for the lighting of the menorah. As he pulled up to the front of the house he noticed their car was not in the driveway. He was certain they'd be home for this holiest of days. He rang the front door bell. He hoped, now with some success under his belt, that his father would be more supportive of his art career.

His mother Helen answered the front door, "Hunter, how good of you to come!"

"Good to see you Mom. Where's Dad?"

"He went to buy new candles. I told him we could use the ones from last year but he said that wasn't kosher. He wanted new ones."

Hunter was about to step inside when he saw his dad pull into the driveway.

"Mmm, something smells good in here. What's cooking, Mom?"

"I'm frying the bimuelos for later."

Steve came through the back door into the kitchen. "Helen, the bimuelos are burning!"

Helen ran into the kitchen and looked in the pot. "No they're not."

"Smelled like they were. I saw Hunter's car out in front."

"Yes, he just got here. He's in the living room."

Steve proceeded to the living room and gave Hunter a hug. "So, how's the artist?"

"Doing pretty good this year. My shows have been very successful, and I've got more lined up in the new year."

"Yeah, yeah, two shows and you think you're Picasso."

"Steve, stop it!" Helen yelled from the kitchen. She was tired of the sarcasm.

When dinner was ready, Helen called the men away from the football game to the dining room table. "What else in happening in your life, Hunter?" his mom asked. "You've mentioned your next door neighbor, Janet. Anything going on with the two of you?"

"Janet is a marketing expert, so she's helping me line up the shows and get acquainted with gallery managers, that's all. We're not going together or anything."

"So to what else do you attribute all this SUCCESS? his dad asked.

Hunter did his best to ignore the continued sarcasm. "Well I'm really grateful to the old couple in the apartment next to mine. Bob and Clara Gerber have been really supportive. In fact, we joke about how they've become the President and CEO of Hunter Art Incorporated."

"How old are they?" Steve asked.

"I'm not sure. In their eighties at least. And we just got some terrible news at our last meeting. Bob just got back from the doctor and found out he's got cancer."

"Oh dear, did he say what stage?" Helen asked.

"He said it has metastasized. But he doesn't want any chemotherapy."

"Oh dear. Oh dear," his mom sighed.

"So, what's he gonna do?" his dad frowned.

"He's probably gonna die," Hunter replied.

"Well that's pretty depressing. Why don't we change the subject," Dad suggested.

Later that evening they lit the menorah and prayed. His mom presented Hunter with a small box. Hunter opened it and was delighted with the gift, several brushes and a palette knife.

Christmas Day dawned sunny and cold. Janet headed to her parents' home in Milwaukee. Hunter stood at his easel, opened some acrylics, mixed them with his new palette knife, and began painting. That afternoon he took a break for dinner and fixed himself a sandwich. It was dark when he finally put the paints away. He glanced at his phone and saw that it was 6:15. I'll just have time to clean up and change clothes before going over to Janet's. I'm sure she said seven o'clock.

Hunter was greeted at Janet's door by Bob. He nodded toward the kitchen. "The women are busy getting things ready. Good to see you, Hunter. How was the visit with your parents?"

"It went okay."

"Were they excited about your shows and all the sales you've had?"

"Not really." Hunter thought back to his dad's comments and wished things were different.

"Sorry to hear that. They should be extremely proud of what you've accomplished the past few months."

"Yeah, but they're not." Hunter was uncomfortable and changed the subject. "By the way, how are you feeling?"

"Pretty good," Bob replied. "I get tired real easily. I've been sleeping a lot. Other than that, I'm doing okay."

"C'mon guys! Have a seat. The coffee and dessert are ready. And I want to hear about everyone's Christmas." Clara was her usual bossy and loveable self.

"I know we said we wouldn't talk about business," Hunter said as he took a seat. "But I want everyone to know I've lined up two more shows in the new year. ENVISION is showing my work in February, and Nathan wants me to show again in April."

"Congratulations! Hunter. I'm so happy for you," Clara responded.

"Me too. I'm proud of the work you're doing, even while you keep painting," Bob added.

"I'll share more details at our next meeting," Hunter responded smiling.

"And you've done it without my help this past month," Janet said proudly.

"Yeah, but you got me started and showed me what to do," Hunter smiled.

"Merry Christmas to both of you," Bob cheered. "Let's eat!"

CHAPTER THIRTEEN

MAN FEEDING PIGEONS

O n December 29th Chicago was hit with a blizzard. The streets were thick with snow. Clean-up would take at least a day or two. Many businesses closed until after New Year's Day. Janet was coming down with a terrible cold. She called Bob and Clara to talk about their meeting on Sunday. "Yes, I'm absolutely miserable. I'm taking a week off from work. Really burned out. I plan to go to bed, eat nothing but hot soup, and sleep until I'm better."

"That's a good plan, Janet," Clara responded. "And there's no reason we have to meet this Sunday night. We were together on Christmas, so let's just meet the third Sunday in January."

"Sounds good to me, and I think Hunter will be okay with that."

"I'll call Hunter and explain what's happening. You take care of yourself and get better quick. Tell you what, I'll bring a big pot of chicken noodle soup to you tomorrow night."

"Oh Clara, you're a dear." Janet was so grateful for such a compassionate neighbor.

With no show planned in January, Hunter was relieved to

have the month of January to himself. The show at Maple Street Gallery had provided a good income from paintings sold. He was ready to report to his friends at the meeting on Sunday. He woke up last week with a scene in mind he wanted to paint. He sketched the main figure, an old beggar standing in front of the park bench. He envisioned this as a sequel to the old man asleep on the bench. The sun is up a little higher than in the first painting, the rays shine brightly through the park trees. The man is awake now and holding a bag with his left hand. With his right hand he is scattering bread crumbs on the grass in front of him; and the pigeons, now about ten of them, are gathered on the ground picking at the bread. The sunshine lights up the flock of pigeons giving one the feeling that hope is alive, in the form of a beggar who is willing to share his bread. *Man Feeding Pigeons*, a painting of hope is just what the Gerbers need right now.

When he began the painting, Hunter knew he was doing this for the Gerbers. It would be a perfect match to the *Man on the Bench* which they had purchased. But this one would be a gift. He wouldn't take a dime. They had done so much for him. Each morning when he began painting, tears came to his eyes thinking about Bob, and wondering how much longer Bob would live. Now it is Saturday and it's obvious the painting won't be finished before their meeting tomorrow night. The phone rang.

"Hello," he answered.

"Hello, Hunter. This is Clara Gerber. I'm calling to let you know we won't be meeting tomorrow night."

"Well that's fine with me. I really don't have anything new to report. How's Bob?"

"Oh, tired as usual. And I think he's getting weaker. But right now, it's Janet I'm worried about. She's come down with a terrible cold."

"Aw, Janet has an owwie." Hunter couldn't resist harkening back to his fall. "There's a lot of flu going around this year. Wasn't that a snowstorm yesterday?"

"It certainly was. I'm glad Bob and I don't have to go out. I think Janet is just burned out from her long hours at work."

"Yeah, lots of pressure. I'm sure she needs a break."

After the phone call Hunter returned to his easel, picked up the brush. He stared at the old man and the pigeons and a tear ran down his cheek. I knew I couldn't finish the painting this week. Now I've got two more weeks to get it done. Janet's sick. Bob's dying. And all I can do is paint.

A week later, it was finished. The details on the trees. The highlights on the bench. A touch of gray to lengthen the old man's hair. Hunter stepped back and gazed admiringly at the finished work. The rays of sunshine; that's what moved him. The canvas was the same size as his previous piece, and he had purchased a matching frame. What a gift this will be! And there is still another week until their meeting.

On Monday evening the phone rang. Bill Anderson from ENVISION called to secure the February dates, and to confirm set up on January 30. No sooner was the call ended when the phone rang again. It was Janet. She was getting over her cold and going back to work. She was calling to check in and ask about the show at ENVISION. "Funny you should ask," Hunter responded. "I just got through talking with Bill."

"Is everything okay?" she asked.

"We've got all the details worked out. I set up on January 30. Show ends February 27."

"Excellent! Now we've got to get to work on March and April."

"C'mon, Janet, one thing at a time."

"Uh-uh, not in marketing. Three things at a time and two steps ahead of the competition."

"That's why you're in marketing and I'm an artist," Hunter laughed.

"I think I've heard that one before."

"All joking aside, I'm glad you're feeling better," Hunter said.

"Thanks, me too. Now get to work!"

Hunter got to work putting the canvas into the frame. I think the Gerbers will love it. Just as he finished, the phone rang again, the third call this evening.

"Hello, Hunter, it's me, Clara. I'm sorry to trouble you. I'm calling from Bob's hospital room."

"Oh, no! What happened?"

"Well, I took him to his doctor appointment this morning. The doctor checked his vitals and shook his head. 'You're going to the hospital,' was all he said. Bob asked him, 'Am I dying?' And the doctor laughed and said, 'No, not today. We just need to get you rehydrated, and get your blood oxygen levels up, and check a few more things.'"

"I'll be right there," Hunter replied.

"No, no, no. That's not necessary," Clara insisted. "I just wanted you to know."

"I want to come. See you in a little while. Say hi to Bob."

"If you do come, I'm sure Bob would be happy to see you."

The painting. The *Man Feeding Pigeons*. Should I take it with me? She said he wasn't going to die today. I'm anxious for them to see it, but I think I'll wait until he comes home. Please, Bob, don't die. Hunter put on his coat and headed out the door. At the hospital, the lights were dim in Bob's room. Hunter leaned over the bed and gave him a hug. He sat in a chair next to Clara who was knitting. Hunter smiled and thought to himself, I should have brought my knitting.

CHAPTER FOURTEEN

THE GIFT IS GIVEN

A few days later Bob was released from the hospital, weak but glad to be home. On Sunday he was feeling well enough to host the Board of Directors. As usual Janet was a few minutes early and was seated on the sofa talking with Clara and Bob about his hospitalization and recovery. They heard a knock at the door. It was Hunter.

"Good evening, Clara, how's Bob doing?"

"Pretty good. We're just so glad to be home. C'mon in." As Hunter walked in she asked, "What's that big wrapped package you're carrying?"

"It's something I did for you and Bob," he replied. Hunter walked into the living room and set the wrapped painting in front of Bob. He said hello to Janet, as Bob started to unwrap the painting.

"Oh my Lord, what is this?" Bob asked with astonishment. He peeled back the paper and lifted the painting from the floor. "Oh my, oh my," he said shaking his head.

"What is it, dear? We can't see it," Clara was dying of curiosity.

"My, oh my," Bob repeated. He slowly turned the painting toward Clara and Janet.

"I call it *Man Feeding Pigeons*," Hunter stated. There was a long silence as they examined the painting, studying the light and the details of the scene.

"Oh, Hunter, it's beautiful!" Clara declared.

"Oh it is," Janet added, "This has got to be one of your best ever!"

"I really like it," Bob agreed. "How much are you asking for it?"

"I told you, it's for you and Clara. It's a gift."

"A gift?" Clara asked. "For us?"

"Yes. You've both done so much for me. I don't know how to thank you, so I was hoping you'd like it."

"Oh, we do!" Clara responded. "We most certainly do!"

"I think we'll hang it in our bedroom next to our other prize," Bob said proudly.

"I'd be honored if you did," Hunter replied.

The conversation eventually turned to the business of Hunter's art shows. He reported on his sales for the past year, and gave another report on the upcoming show at ENVISION. Janet inquired about other galleries and promised to help line up new shows for the rest of the year. She turned to Clara and smiled. "Do you remember several months ago suggesting we get a website for Hunter's work?"

"I remember, but I thought you'd forgotten," Clara replied.

"Oh no. I didn't forget. I just had it on the back burner because we were so busy meeting gallery owners and managers. Well . . . it's time for us to get started. I've got some ideas, but I also want Hunter to be a part of the development of the website."

"I don't have a clue about website development, but I guess I could learn."

"That's the spirit, my boy," Bob interjected. "Janet is willing to help you, but you've got to be willing to accept her input."

"Yeah, I know . . . and be grateful."

"Now you're talkin'," Bob was so pleased to see Hunter responding well to their efforts.

There was a little more discussion about Bob's time in the hospital. Then Hunter and Janet said good night to the Gerbers and returned to their apartments.

CHAPTER FIFTEEN

MELANOMA

Hunter spent most of the day, January 30th, setting up his show at ENVISION. He and Bill Anderson discussed where each painting would be hung, how they would be grouped and lit. It was getting dark early as the last piece was put in place. Bill did a preliminary adjustment to the lights before turning them all on. "Ready?" he asked Hunter. Bill began throwing switches and the gallery was flooded with light.

"Wow!" Hunter declared. "This is great!"

"I'll make some final adjustments focusing the lights and we'll be ready for opening night. Why don't you drop by tomorrow just to check everything one more time? But remember, the day after tomorrow is the first. I hope you'll be here that evening, and on the weekend as well."

"I wouldn't miss it. And thank you for showing my work. And thank you for all your time today." Hunter shook Bill's hand with sincere appreciation.

On opening night, the first patron to enter the gallery was

Janet accompanied by Bob and Clara. Hunter and Bill welcomed them warmly and began the tour of the two rooms full of Hunter's paintings. Later that evening as the gallery was closing, Bill pulled Hunter aside and shared the news . . . "Three sales so far, and one strong possibility for later."

"Fantastic!" Hunter bid Bill a good night and promised to be back on Saturday.

Two more paintings were sold, one on Saturday and another on Sunday. Hunter was pleased, and visiting with Bill during the show helped pass the time.

"Hunter, why do you keep scratching your shoulder?" Bill asked.

"It itches," he replied.

Bill ignored the scratching for a while but as the evening progressed Hunter kept scratching.

"Maybe you don't realize it, but you've been scratching all evening."

"Yeah, it's really bothering me. Maybe a mosquito bite."

"Not likely this time of year."

"Could be something else in my apartment," Hunter suggested.

"Do you mind if I take a look?" Bill asked.

Hunter looked around and saw only one couple in the gallery. The two of them moved around the corner into the other room for a little privacy. Hunter unbuttoned his shirt and pulled the sleeve down. "I can't see back there."

"Let me see," Bill replied. "Hmm, that looks strange."

"What is it?"

"I'm not sure, but it's bumpy and dark brown."

"Now that I think about it, it's been itching for a week or more."

"Maybe you should get it checked," Bill urged.

"Yeah, I probably should." Hunter was thinking about his lack of medical insurance, and how he hated to go to the doctor.

"I think I've seen pictures of skin cancer that look bumpy like that," Bill added.

"Yeah, I'll call somebody tomorrow and see when I can get in."

A short time later Hunter bid Bill a good night. The gallery was empty. Bill turned out the lights and locked up. The first few days had gone extremely well.

Monday morning Hunter twisted his shoulders around in the bathroom, trying to see the back of his shoulder in the mirror. It hurt his neck, but the brown spot was disturbing to see. After shaving and brushing his teeth, he began researching on line for skin doctors and finally got an appointment for the end of the week.

The doctor asked Hunter to remove all his clothing and don a loose-fitting hospital gown. Soon the doctor returned for a total body inspection. "Well, the good news is there is only one spot. The bad news is that it is definitely a melanoma," the doctor announced. "The sooner we get that removed, the better."

"Do you think you could do it today?" Hunter asked.

"We do have time, if you're willing to proceed," the doctor replied.

"Let's get it done," Hunter answered.

The procedure took longer than Hunter expected. And it hurt. The local anesthesia seemed to be working at first, but the deeper the incision, the more it hurt. The doctor explained why he was cutting so much tissue, and that a sample would be sent to the hospital lab for testing. "We'll have the results in a couple of days, but I'm sure that's a melanoma."

"Will you have to do any more cutting?" Hunter asked grimacing.

"I don't think so. I went pretty deep. You will have to come back in a couple of weeks so I can check the stitches and see how your wound is doing. My assistant will schedule the follow-up before you leave. It's a good thing you came in when you did."

"I'm glad to have it over," Hunter said with a smile.

"I'll want to check you again in six months, and again at a year," the doctor added.

"Why's that?" Hunter asked.

"Just to make sure there is no recurrence, and that it hasn't metastasized."

"Oh, okay, thanks, doc." As the doctor left the examining room, Hunter dressed and prepared to leave. He was about to depart when the nurse met him at the door with a post-visit summary and appointment for a week from Friday.

Back at the apartment, Hunter couldn't wait to talk to Bob and Clara. As they opened their door, Hunter said, "Guess what?"

They could tell he was excited. "What?" They replied together.

"I've got cancer too!"

"No!" Clara shouted. Her face turned wild with panic.

"No, no, not that kind of cancer," Hunter tried to calm her. "Not what Bob has. I just had a spot of melanoma removed from my shoulder."

"Are you okay?" Bob asked.

"Yeah, I just got back from the doctor and he removed the spot from my shoulder. It is kinda sore. He had to cut pretty deep."

"Oh, Hunter, I'm so sorry," Clara grabbed his hand. "Did he get it all?"

"He's pretty sure he did. I've got a follow-up visit in a couple weeks. I just thought it was an amazing coincidence that Bob and I both have cancer at the same time."

"We'll be cancer brothers," Bob replied. "And we'll pray for each other."

"You better believe it," Hunter said. "I'm just so thankful mine could be treated."

"Amen, brother," Bob said and stretched out his arms to give Hunter a hug.

CHAPTER SIXTEEN

JANET'S PROMOTION

The February show at ENVISION was a huge success. Hunter was becoming more comfortable with his time at the galleries. His confidence was growing along with his income. He became good friends with Bill Anderson, and thanked him for urging him to see the doctor about his shoulder scratching. Bill was glad to hear the melanoma was gone.

February also marked the launching of Hunter's website. Janet had a little free time and offered to help Hunter set it up. At their monthly meeting, Hunter asked the Gerbers' permission to use *Man Feeding Pigeons* on his home web page.

"Do you want it back?" Clara asked.

"Oh no," Hunter replied. "I have a copy of it on my computer. I just want to use the photo for my website."

"Hunter and I both agreed it would make a great centerpiece," Janet added, "and if anyone inquires, we can say it's already been sold."

JIM BORNZIN

"But we didn't buy it," Clara replied, "Hunter gave it to us as a gift."

"No one needs to know that," Janet responded with a smile.

"Of course, you have our permission," Bob replied. "Anything we can do to help."

After several evenings together working on Hunter's computer, the website was launched. Twenty of his best works were shown with prices listed. Hunter couldn't believe how much Janet said they were worth. She explained, "This is just a platform to show people a sample of what's available at your shows. If they purchase directly from you, you won't have to give the galleries a cut. Right? And this tab on your home page takes people to the listing of current and future gallery exhibits. And the galleries will appreciate the link you've provided to their gallery websites."

"Wow, I can't believe I've got my own website," Hunter turned from the screen to look into Janet's eyes. "You really know what you're doing. I can't thank you enough."

"Your enthusiasm is thanks enough," Janet smiled in return. "Next month, we'll get you up and running on social media."

"I already Facebook with some of my friends," Hunter replied.

"That's a good start, but I'll show you ways to reach a wider community."

"What about the webpage? Can't people just look at that?" Hunter asked.

"Yes, but social media will help you communicate more directly, and will drive people to the website. And remember, you'll have to update the website each month to keep it fresh."

"Oh, oh. Now I'm getting that creepy feeling again. I'll be so busy marketing my art on the computer that I won't have time to paint."

"Or," Janet argued, "you'll make a schedule for yourself. Personally, I couldn't live without my schedule. You'll set aside time each week for promoting your art, which will make time at the easel even more precious."

Hunter looked askance, "You know, sometimes you almost make sense."

Janet was excited for Hunter and excited about her work as well. She saw how much her skill and experience had meant to her neighbor. Her relationship with others in the office seemed more important, and she felt a sense of energy about her work. She hadn't felt depressed for months. Her job was not just about selling the product, it was about helping everyone succeed.

Suddenly it was March. As Janet looked at her calendar, she realized she and Hunter needed to confirm the shows coming up at Nathan's gallery in April, and hopefully, at Brightside again in May. They also needed to update the website, and Hunter would need more guidance on Facebook and Twitter. She smiled as she thought back to last March, a year ago. Last year she was so tired of winter, so tired of work, so anxious, and so depressed. She remembered the long evenings watching, but not enjoying, TV programs; and the even longer nights of restless sleep. This year her calendar was full of meetings at work and meetings with Hunter, gallery events, evenings with the Gerbers, and evenings with co-workers. What's happening to me? I'm not that interested in art. And yet, something has changed.

One evening she brought dinner to the Gerbers, anxious to hear how Bob was doing. Clara welcomed her warmly and helped her carry several bowls from Janet's apartment. Bob was asleep in his old recliner and snoring rather loudly. She observed he had lost more weight, a mere skeleton of his former vigorous self. She and Clara got the table set and the food in place. Clara went to Bob and tried to wake him.

"Bob . . . Bob . . it's time to get up. Janet brought us dinner and everything is ready."

Bob opened his eyes, looked around slowly. Janet wondered if he knew where he was.

"C'mon, honey, give me your hand. I'll help you up."

Bob struggled to get out of the recliner and leaned on Clara as they moved to the table.

"Hello, Bob," Janet smiled and shook Bob's feeble hand.

After they were seated, Bob said, "Let us pray. Heavenly Father we thank you for this meal. Bless the hands that prepared it and strengthen us for thy service, in Jesus' name. Amen"

As the bowls were passed Clara smiled at Janet and said to Bob, "Did you know Janet prepared this meal?"

"No, but it all looks good."

They ate quietly, and after dinner, Bob returned to his recliner while Clara and Janet cleared the table and washed the dishes. Janet picked up the towel and began to dry the plates and silverware. Tears were streaming down Clara's cheeks. "I don't think he'll last much longer."

"He is certainly weaker than last month," Janet agreed. When the dishes were done, Janet returned to her apartment, checked her emails, said a prayer for Bob and Clara, and went to bed.

A few days later the vice-president of marketing called Janet into the office. The new year had begun well. Janet couldn't imagine what the problem might be.

"Have a seat, Janet," her boss said. "I'll get right to the point."

Janet was really nervous now. She could tell his tone was serious.

"You're being offered a promotion. You can have a week to consider whether or not you want to accept it. After you let me know, we'll make the announcement company-wide."

"A promotion?" Janet wasn't sure what to say. She wasn't sure she could allow herself to shift from anxious fear to excited joy.

"Yes, you've been chosen to fill the position of Director of Marketing in our Los Angeles office."

"You're not joking?"

"No, of course not. The position will pay $160,000. But, of course, you'll have to move. Are you interested?"

"Yes, yes I am. I'm definitely interested." Janet tried to sound professional.

"Good. As I said, think about if for a week before making a final decision. And congratulations!"

CHAPTER SEVENTEEN

JANET'S FAREWELL

It was an offer she couldn't refuse. In the middle of a Chicago winter, sunny California sounded awfully good . . and a hundred and sixty didn't sound bad either. Her parents were actually excited for her when she told them the news. She hoped they would be. The difficult part of moving would be leaving the Hunter Art Corporation. These crazy apartment friends had become family to Janet and saying good-by would not be easy. Clara Gerber heard the news with sadness in her heart, but told Janet she was so happy for her. "Why don't we have one more meeting of the Hunter Art group just for old times' sake?" she asked Janet.

"I'd love that," Janet replied, "but will Bob be okay? Will it be too much for him?"

"I'm sure he'll want to celebrate your promotion, and say good-by. I've been trying not to think about Bob's passing. It helped to know I had you and Hunter to lean on. Now, you'll be gone too."

"That's what makes it so hard for me," Janet responded. "The two of you have been so good to me. I wish I could be here when

Bob leaves our world, but I know he would want me to accept this promotion."

"Yes, he would, dear," Clara took Janet's hand and squeezed it tightly.

"I'll notify Hunter," Janet said, "and I'll bring refreshments. See you Sunday night."

Bob was asleep in his recliner when Janet came to their apartment. In her arms she carried the dessert she had promised to bring. A few minutes later Hunter knocked at the door and Janet went to let him in. The two frenemies stared at each other for a moment. Janet considered giving him a hug, but he was carrying a large wrapped package, probably another of his paintings. "Come in," she said and stepped back.

Hunter set the package against the sofa and leaned down to Bob and put a hand on his shoulder. "Time to wake up, old man. You've got to call this meeting to order."

Bob opened his eyes and smiled. "Well, look who's here."

Janet stepped over and gave him a hug. "Good to see you, Mr. Chairman of the Board."

Clara looked lovingly at her husband, "Bob, can I get you anything?"

He waved his hand weakly in reply, "No, but you can all take a seat. It's time to get on with business." As they sat in their familiar places he continued, "The final meeting of the Hunter Art Corporation will now come to order. I understand one of our members will be leaving soon. Janet, is there anything you wish to say?"

Choking back tears, Janet realized there were two members leaving, both she and Bob would soon be gone. "You guys have become such a part of my life. I don't know how to thank you for all you've done for me." She paused, then turned to Hunter, "Yeah, you too." They all broke into laughter. "As you all know, I've been offered a promotion, a big raise and a move to California. I can't turn it down. You three are the only reason I'd consider staying here in Chicago."

"You can't do that, young lady," Bob spoke up.

"But we're sure going to miss you," Clara added.

"And that includes me," Hunter contributed.

"No more than I will miss the three of you. In fact, I've been thinking, it's because of you I got this promotion."

"How could that be?" Hunter asked puzzled.

Janet smiled and looked at each of them. "You may not know this, but last year, I was in a real funk. I was depressed and wondering what on earth I was living for. Then I met you.

Actually, I think it was that night Hunter tripped on the stairs, remember? Clara gave us our marching orders that started this whole thing. Remember?"

"How could I forget? This knee still hurts sometimes from the cold." Hunter rubbed his knee in remembrance.

"I had no time for that good-for-nothing artist," Janet continued. "I couldn't believe Clara telling me I had to show him how to market his paintings."

Clara interjected, "So are you saying you needed him as much as he needed you?"

"I didn't realize it at the time, but yes, I needed him." She fixed her gaze on Hunter, "I needed you."

Hunter was struck dumb. He couldn't speak. He didn't know what to say. No one had ever needed him. He stared at Janet, whom he had hated and admired since he first saw her. His eyes dropped to the package at his knees. He reached down and slowly handed the gift to her.

"Oh, Hunter, no," Janet said as she carefully received the painting. Clara and Bob looked on smiling. Janet gently tore off the paper wrapping. "Oh, Hunter . . ." and she began to cry.

Clara rose from her chair, and moved toward Janet who handed her the painting. Clara looked at it and carried it to Bob. "Look what Hunter did for Janet," she said lovingly to her husband.

"That's beautiful," Bob said, admiring the art. "That's a young woman dancing wildly. Who was your model?" Bob asked smiling.

"Well, I didn't have a model exactly," Hunter answered sheepishly, "but Janet was my inspiration."

"I like the way she is leaping from the floor, and the way all the bright colors and light are spinning around her," Bob continued.

"It's like all this energy is just flowing from her," Clara added, looking at Hunter.

"Yeah, that's what I was trying to capture," Hunter replied.

Janet rose from her chair, wiped her eyes with her handkerchief, and stood in front of Hunter. Hunter stood up, and they hugged. It was a long, warm, wonderful hug. Nothing sexual, just the most amazing, loving hug he had ever received. "Thank you," Janet whispered in his ear.

"Thank you," he whispered to her.

The following week Hunter drove Janet to O'Hare. They were met near the airline check-in counter by her parents from Milwaukee. Janet introduced them to Hunter, and with hugs all around, Janet moved through the security queue toward the gate. They waited until she cleared the TSA official. She turned and waved good-by before disappearing down the concourse.

CHAPTER EIGHTEEN

BROTHER RALPH

Janet could hardly believe the California dream. Sixty five degrees in mid-March? It only took her a couple of weeks to find the cutest house, just south of downtown L.A. She worked hard getting to know everyone in her new office. After meeting people in the corporation, or clients of her company, she would discreetly make notes, take them home and review them each evening.

In addition to her promotion, Janet was excited to re-connect with her brother, Ralph and his family. They lived in San Jose, about 350 miles from LA. It would be a five or six hour drive from her cozy home in South Park. A month after settling into her new place, Janet called Ralph one evening. She could hear his daughter and son fighting in the background.

"Just a minute," he said to Janet, then turned and yelled at the kids. "Go fight in the bedroom!" The squabbling faded as the children left the room. "Welcome to California, Jan. Mom told me you were coming out here with a new job."

"Not exactly a new job. I'm working for the same company, just a different region."

"Have you found a place to live?"

"Yes, I've got a cozy place in south Los Angeles."

"When are you coming up to San Jose?"

"I was wondering if Easter weekend would be okay?"

"Don't see why not. I'll tell Trish you're coming."

"Do you have room for a guest? Or should I book a hotel room?"

"You can sleep in Jeff's room, and he can sleep on the floor in a sleeping bag in his sister's room."

"Are you sure that will work?"

"We'll make it work."

"Then I'll plan to drive up on Saturday."

"Sounds good."

As Easter approached, Janet began planning her visit. She had her overnight bag packed, along with small gifts for Jeff and Julie. She left early Saturday morning, hoping the traffic wouldn't be too bad on I-5. North of L.A. it was smooth sailing. She was hungry but didn't want to stop to eat. She was anxious to see her brother. Janet arrived at her brother's shortly before 1 pm.

Ralph answered the door and invited her inside. The kids were screaming at each other and the house was a mess.

"Where's Trish?" Janet asked.

"In Colorado visiting her sister," Ralph replied. "Kids, stop it!" He yelled.

"When will she be back?"

"Go to the bedroom!" he yelled again. Jeff yanked the doll from Julie's hands and she screamed an ear-piercing scream. Ralph grabbed Jeff by the arm and started pulling him toward the bedroom. Jeff dropped the doll. Ralph almost threw Jeff into the bedroom and slammed the door. Julie picked up the doll and ran into her parents' bedroom and jumped on the bed.

"Where were we?" Ralph asked Janet.

Janet was upset by what she had witnessed but tried to play it cool. "I asked when Trish will be back from Colorado."

"Have a seat," Ralph motioned toward the sofa. "I don't really know. She's been gone a week now. I called her at her sister's yesterday and she hung up on me. We've been having a lot of problems."

"Oh, Ralph, I'm sorry to hear that." Janet was at a loss for words.

"It all started last summer. Trish found out I was seeing someone."

"Oh, Ralph. No."

"I broke off the relationship, but I guess the damage was already done."

"I don't know what to say," Janet shook her head in sympathy and disgust.

"Now the kids are really upset with their mom gone."

"Maybe this isn't the best time for me to be visiting," Janet offered.

Ralph shrugged his shoulders.

"Is there anything I can do?" Janet asked.

Ralph thought for a moment. "No, not really."

"Maybe I should go. We'll talk when things settle down, and I'll come another time."

"Maybe that would be best," Ralph agreed.

Janet rose and they hugged good-by. On the drive back to L.A. she cried.

This was not how it was supposed to be, seeing her brother again. She promised herself she would call every week to check in. And she hoped Trish could forgive him and come home. In the meantime, she had her work and plenty of challenges there. She'd try not to think too often about Ralph, and Jeff and Julie. But darn it! It hurt.

CHAPTER NINETEEN

EVERYTHING CHANGES

"Hello," Janet answered on the second ring.

"Hi, Janet. This is Hunter."

"Oh, hi! How are you?"

"Pretty good. I've got a good report to share. Nathan showed my work in April, and I got another showing at Brightside this month."

"Congratulations! So glad to hear you're doing well. I sure love the *Dancing Girl* you gave me. It's hanging above the fireplace in my living room."

"Are you liking your new job?" Hunter asked.

"Yes I am. The people in the office here are great. We've got a fantastic marketing team. It's hard to believe I've been here three months already."

"Yeah, I'm sorry I haven't called more often," Hunter apologized.

"No problem. I've been so busy. Sorry I haven't called you. By the way, how are the Gerbers?"

"Well, that's the other reason I'm calling."

"Bob?" she asked with anticipation.

"Yeah." Hunter paused. "Passed away last night."

"I'm so sorry to hear that. He was such a dear man. How's Clara?"

"Oh, you know Clara. I can tell she's really sad. But nothing seems to stop her."

"Yes, she's an amazing woman," Janet said with admiration.

"There's gonna be a memorial service next Saturday. Do you think you could come?"

"Oh, Hunter. I wish I could. But I'm so swamped here. I promise I'll call Clara."

"That'd be nice." A long pause.

"And I'll send a sympathy card with a note," Janet added.

"So did you find a nice place to live?" Hunter asked.

"Yes, I did. It's a very small older home, in a nice little neighborhood. Do you remember the cartoon TV show called 'South Park'?"

"Yeah, the characters were crazy kids," Hunter replied.

"Well my house is actually in an area called South Park, just south of downtown LA."

"South Park. That's funny. How long does it take you to get to work?"

"Only about twenty minutes, and in L.A. that's pretty good."

"I'm glad you like your painting," Hunter continued. "I'll tell Clara I talked to you."

"Thanks, Hunter. And thanks for calling about Bob. Tell Clara I miss her."

"Sure will. G'bye."

The memorial service on Saturday was held at the Senior Center just a few blocks up the street. Hunter was surprised to see so many people in attendance. Several older people stood up to say what they remembered about Bob, his kindness, his sense of humor, the wisdom he loved to share. Hunter considered speaking, but as emotional as he felt, he couldn't bring himself to do it. He hung around after the luncheon, and when nearly everyone was gone, he walked with Clara back to their apartment building.

"I talked with Janet earlier this week. She said to tell you she was sorry she couldn't come today. She said she really misses you."

"Thank you, Hunter. Yes, she called me yesterday and apologized for not coming."

"She thinks the world of you and Bob," Hunter smiled.

"She's a dear. I do miss her." After a moment Clara shook her finger at Hunter. "Now don't you go moving away!"

"I won't. I won't." Hunter couldn't help but chuckle.

The weeks that followed were hard for both of them. Hunter and Clara greeted each other on the stairs some days, and some days at the mail boxes.

"I got another show lined up at Vertical Gallery," Hunter boasted. "That's one of the best in the city."

"I've heard of that one," Clara responded. "Congratulations!"

"It's not until July, so I'll have a free month to do some new pieces for their show."

"Don't let me keep you from your work," Clara grinned as she headed up the stairs.

During June they didn't see much of each other. Hunter was busy painting. Clara walked occasionally to the Senior Center to play Bingo. Her heart was broken, no wonder her chest hurt.

Today the sun was shining and after skimming through the catalogs that came in the mail, she threw her shawl over her shoulders and headed up the street. Lunch was served promptly at noon at the Center, so she was walking as fast as she could. Ah, I made it. Clara grabbed the railing and started up the stairs. Almost to the doors. She collapsed. Her friend Penny, waiting inside, saw her face through the door window, and waited to watch her enter, but she didn't. Penny walked to the door and pushed it open. There was Clara, lying on the cement just in front of the door.

Penny gasped and ran to tell the staff in the office. "Clara Gerber collapsed and is lying by the front door!" she hollered. They called 9-1-1. Penny ran back to Clara and knelt over her. Clara was barely able to talk but couldn't get up.

The ambulance arrived in less than five minutes. The paramedics checked her pulse and prepared to shock her, but it wasn't necessary. Her pulse was irregular but steady. They loaded her on a gurney, started the IV, and transported her to Chicago General Hospital. At the hospital, Clara was stabilized but kept under fairly heavy sedation, allowing her heart to rest.

A couple of days later she woke in CCU and asked the nurse what happened. "You were walking to the Senior Center and collapsed on the stairs," the nurse explained. "You've had a pretty serious heart attack, but you're stable now."

"You mean, I almost died?" Clara asked.

"Well, almost. But the paramedics got there in time."

"How long have I been in the hospital?"

"Today is your third day here. Is there someone we should notify?"

Clara thought for a moment. "My friend Penny."

"According to your chart, that's who made the call for the ambulance."

"Oh, and my friend Hunter," Clara added. "He lives in the same apartment building."

"Do you know his number?" the nurse asked.

"No, but you could look it up. His name is Hunter Schlewitz."

"We'll let him know you're here."

Hunter showed up that evening carrying a large cloth bag.

"What've you got in there?" Clara asked.

"Well, the nurse told me on the phone that you had a heart attack, but now you're stable and sitting up and eating on your own."

"What's in the bag?" Clara asked again.

"I never thought I'd tell anyone, but I know I can trust you," Hunter said smiling.

"Are you gonna tell me, or just keep torturing me?" Clara chided. "What's in the bag?"

Hunter opened the bag and pulled out a ball of yarn and two knitting needles.

"My knitting!" Clara exclaimed.

"No. MY knitting needles," Hunter replied. "I couldn't get into your apartment to get your knitting needles, so I brought mine."

"You knit?" Clara asked incredulous.

"Sure do," Hunter said boldly. "But don't you dare tell anyone!"

"Why Hunter Schlewitz, there are still things I'm learning about you."

"Well, see, I get tired of painting sometimes and need a break. So I discovered I could sit in the living room or kitchen and knit for a while, and think about my painting. It kind of clears my head, if you know what I mean."

"I most certainly do. Knitting allows me to think about a lot of things and still accomplish something worthwhile," Clara said knowingly. "And don't you worry. I won't tell a soul."

Hunter sat down and they visited for about half an hour. During a lull in the conversation Clara closed her eyes. "Well, Clara, I don't want to tire you out. Why don't you have the nurse call me when they're ready to discharge you?"

"Okay, I will. Thank you, Hunter. Come here. Give me a hug before you go."

Back at his apartment, Hunter reviewed the events of the past several months. Janet's leaving. Bob's passing. And now, Clara's heart attack. Could things get any worse? At least my art business is going well. I've done some good work lately. And I've got a show at the Vertical Gallery. Never dreamed that could happen. Thanks to Janet. Thanks to the Gerbers.

CHAPTER TWENTY

CLARA'S SURRISE

Clara was really excited about leaving the Cardiac Care Unit. The nurse came in to give her the news. "Hi, Clara. Our social worker found a really nice place for you."

"Does that mean I'm finally going home?" Clara asked.

"Not exactly. We've determined that because of your weakness you'll have to go to a rehab center for a while."

"But I want to go back to my apartment."

"I'm sorry, that won't be possible. The doctor says you need some place where your medications will be monitored, where you can get some physical therapy, and your meals will be prepared for you."

When Hunter arrived she shared the news with him and gave him the address of her Care Center. They stopped at the apartment first to pick up clothes and her knitting basket. Then Hunter drove her to her new place of residence, at least for the time being. Clara hoped she would be able to return to the apartment in a week or two. Hunter said he hoped so too.

One week passed. Two weeks turned to three. Clara was still very weak. She was beginning to think she may never get back home. Hunter visited once a week, usually on Sunday evening in memory of their old "corporation" meetings. Clara's friend Penny was also making a weekly visit much to Clara's delight.

"Penny, I have an idea, but I need your help to carry it out."

"What can I do for you?" Penny asked.

"I want you to do a little exploring. My friend Hunter has his art on display at the Vertical Gallery on Western Avenue. Go there and ask to speak to the manager or owner of the gallery. Tell him or her that you are a patron of the arts in Chicago and acquainted with Hunter's work. Tell him you own a couple of Hunter's priceless pieces and ask if they ever have an auction. Get as much information as you can about art auctions and report back to me. Okay?"

"Oh, Clara, this sounds like fun." Penny was obviously intrigued.

"Whatever you do, if you run into Hunter, don't tell him a word about this. Okay?"

"Got it! I'm your gal. I'll find out what I can. Mums the word!" And with that, Penny was gone.

A week later, Penny was back. She shared the auction information with Clara, then Clara shared more of her secret plan with Penny. "Now remember, don't say a word to Hunter."

At the end of July, Hunter visited the Care Center with exciting news.

"The Vertical Gallery exhibit was a huge success!" he told Clara. "I sold six of my paintings, and you won't believe what I got for them."

"Well, tell me," Clara begged.

"Some sold for six and eight thousand dollars. Can you believe it?"

"Hunter, that's wonderful! I'm so happy for you."

"Never in my wildest dreams did I think my paintings would be worth that much."

"Bob was right. You can be humble about yourself, and proud of the gifts God has given you. We've always believed in your talent."

"Oh, Clara, I wish Bob was here. I wish Janet was here too. We'd be having one heck of a party."

"Will you visit me again next Sunday?" Clara asked.

"Of course," Hunter answered.

The following Sunday evening Hunter arrived at the Care Center a little after seven p.m. He went to Clara's room and saw the door open and the light on. Clara was sitting in the chair beside her bed waiting for him. Hunter turned the other chair to face her.

"Hi Clara, time for the Hunter Art Corporation meeting!" It was not quite true anymore, but it brought a smile to her face.

"In the absence of Chairman Bob, I hereby call the meeting to order," Clara announced.

"I am sad to report that I have no show lined up for August," Hunter asserted.

"But I have some wonderful news for the corporation this evening," Clara said.

Hunter wondered how Clara could have any news, sitting here in the Care Center all week.

Clara continued, "At the end of July, there was an art auction at the Vertical Gallery."

"Yes, I saw the announcement. But how did you know that?" Hunter said with a puzzled frown.

"And at that auction, two works by Hunter Schlewitz were sold. One for $35,000 and the other for $48,000. They were purchased by the renowned Carl Hammer Gallery which houses one of Chicago's premier collections of modern American artists."

Hunter looked at her and smiled. The old gal is getting senile. He didn't have any paintings up for auction; and if he did, they would never sell for . . . how much did she say? She must be making all this up. How would she know about the Carl Hammer Gallery? "Why Clara, that's wonderful news!" Hunter said with exaggerated joy. "Where did you hear all that?"

"From my friend Penny," Clara answered.

"And who is Penny?" he asked.

"It's kind of a long story. Penny is my friend from the Senior Center, and she's the one who called 9-1-1 when I fell. I owe her my life." Clara gathered her thoughts. "A couple of weeks ago, we learned about the auction at Vertical. I gave Penny the key to my apartment and she went and got your two paintings, *Man on the Bench* and *Man Feeding Pigeons*. She brought them here and I showed them to the manager of the Care Center. Then I asked him to write a contract for me, verifying my ownership of the paintings, and my desire to auction them to the highest bidder at the Vertical Gallery auction. Here is your check for $66,400. I'm sorry they took 20% for their fee." Clara held out the check. "Go on, take it."

Hunter reached out, his hand shaking, and took the check. "But those paintings were for you and Bob," he said weakly.

"Bob is gone, dear. And I'll be with him pretty soon. And I'm not going back to my apartment. And we don't have any children to inherit them. If you want to see them, the address is on the check for the Carl Hammer Gallery. I think it's downtown on North Wells Street."

"Yeah, I've been there. My college art class went there several years ago. They're noted for artists who portray national and ethnic identity, paintings that express the human condition."

"That's probably why they liked *Man on the Bench*. It certainly expresses loneliness and yet, hope."

"I can't believe you did that," Hunter was on the verge of tears as he looked at the check.

"I'm sorry if you're angry. I didn't know what else to do with the paintings. I was hoping you'd be pleased."

"I'm not angry. I'm just overwhelmed by what you've done. I can't believe this check."

"Don't spend it all in one place!" Clara said giggling. "That was one of Bob's sayings."

"Do you need any of this for your care here?" Hunter asked.

"No, dear. I'm fine. As temporary Chairman of the Board I'd like to suggest you look into the possibility of renting or owning your own gallery. Maybe a place with a studio upstairs where you can paint. I'll bet you've never thought of that," Clara smiled again.

"No, I never thought I'd have my own gallery. But I promise . . I'll think about it."

CHAPTER TWENTY-ONE

THE HUNTER GALLERY

It had been a small used clothing store on West Division Street near Humboldt Park. The rent was reasonable and it was only a short bus ride from his apartment. Hunter proudly fastened the new sign above the door: the HUNTER GALLERY. It had been two years since Clara had made the suggestion that he get his own gallery. Hunter had been reluctant to take this risk for several reasons. His income had been decent for the past year. There were six galleries willing to show his work on a regular basis, but sales had slowed, though the value of his paintings had risen. Going into his own gallery meant a different kind of business model, and Janet was no longer around to give him advice.

A year ago Clara moved from the rehab center to a retirement home. Independent Living they called it. She had her own apartment, and the meals they served in the dining room were usually quite good. She was receiving good care, but had become progressively weaker. Hunter cut his visits back to about once a month, usually on a Saturday or Sunday afternoon.

"Clara, guess what I did?" Hunter asked excitedly.

"You got married!" Clara teased.

"No, no, nothing like that! I rented a space for a gallery. The Hunter Gallery!"

"You didn't!"

"Yes I did. It's a small space on West Division. It used to be a clothing store. I'm getting all new lighting. Putting in temporary, moveable walls for display areas. I've got a desk and file cabinet in the back corner where I'll keep all my records. I'm really excited! And to be honest, a little scared."

"Oh, Hunter, I'm so glad for you!"

"Do you remember my friend, Nathan?"

"Yes, I think he was one of the first to show your work, wasn't he?"

"That's right. Well, he's helping me set up my new business venture. He's given me samples of sales orders, receipts, and reviewed all the costs involved in running a gallery."

"And is there a room in back where you can paint?"

"No, the space isn't big enough for that. So for the time being I'll continue to paint at the apartment."

"Who's going to look after the gallery when you're home painting?"

"I've been giving that a lot of thought. I certainly can't afford to hire anyone. I thought I might limit the hours the gallery is open. That will give me more time to paint."

"Here's what I think you should do, Mr. Schlewitz."

"Still giving orders, Mrs. Gerber?"

"Now you listen to me, young man. Here is what WE are going to do. Tuesdays and Thursdays will be MY days at the gallery. Let's say you're open from 10 am to 6 pm. You come and pick me up at 9:45 after I've had breakfast. I'll tell the staff here to pack my lunch. You drop me off at 10 am to open the gallery, and then you go home and paint. At 4:30 you come back to the gallery and take me home. Hang a sign in your window that says, 'Running an errand, back at 5.' You go back to the gallery, review my notes for that day, and lock up at 6.

How does that sound?"

"That's quite an offer, but I told you I can't afford to pay you for all those hours."

"Nonsense! I don't need to be paid! I just need something to do!"

"But Clara, you're very weak, and I'm not sure the doctor would approve of your working. Even one day a week."

"Who said anything about working? I'm just volunteering. And I can sit in a chair at your gallery as comfortably as I can sit here in my room."

"Hmmm." Hunter could hardly believe it sounded so reasonable.

"I should have asked. Is there a restroom in your gallery?" Clara grinned

"Yeah, at the very back."

"Then I guess I'm all set."

It was a crazy idea. But Hunter decided to give it a try. When he first spoke to the nursing staff, he asked permission to take Mrs. Gerber out for part of the day, from noon to 5 pm on Thursday. He figured if that went okay, he would do the same thing the following Tuesday, and sign her out from 10 am to 5 pm.

"You be certain to have her back here by 5 pm," the charge nurse said. "Dinner is served promptly at 5:30."

"Yes, ma'am, promptly back by 5. And we certainly appreciate the staff packing a lunch for her to take out."

"Clara, you have our number here at the office. You be sure to call us if there is any problem or any delay in your return. Do you understand?"

"I most certainly do. Hunter will be taking good care of me." And with that, they were gone.

When they arrived at the gallery, Clara was thrilled to see the Hunter Gallery sign above the door. She pointed up and shouted, "You did it! You really did it!"

"It was your idea, remember?" Hunter gave her a quick hug, pulled the key from his pocket and unlocked the door. Once inside, he turned the door sign to OPEN, and showed Clara to her chair near the front window. "I'm glad you brought your knitting. And

I checked out a couple of books from the library you might enjoy reading."

"Hunter, my boy, you think of everything. Now show me what to do if someone wants to buy one of your paintings."

Hunter showed her the desk and all the necessary forms. "Are you sure you're going to be all right here by yourself?"

"There's a phone right here on the desk. And I see the bathroom door, so I'll be fine. And don't you forget," Clara smiled and paused, "I'm not doing this to help you. I'm doing this because I need an excuse to get out of the 'home.'" The two of them roared with laughter.

Hunter began to believe this might work after all. He was awed again by Clara's great spirit. "You be sure to call me if you have any questions or if you need anything. Okay?"

"I'll be just fine. I'm so excited to have a new adventure. This is going to be fun!"

Hunter could hardly wait to get back to his apartment so he could paint.

CHAPTER TWENTY-TWO

JANET IN CALIFORNIA

Janet's first year in California was filled with success. The western region set new sales records largely because of her contributions to online marketing. Her little home in South Park was home to numerous plants, one cat, and Hunter's painting of the *Dancing Girl*. She loved the California palm trees lining the streets, and month after month of balmy weather. Only the occasional days of Santa Ana winds made it uncomfortable, but at least it blew the smog away. She avoided a couple of requests for dates from single guys at work. Hunter's calls from Chicago were becoming less and less frequent.

"Hi Janet. Thought you might want to have Mrs. Gerber's new address and phone number. She had to move from the rehab center to Independent Living at a big retirement home."

"Thanks Hunter. I'll write that down and give her a call. How are things going for you?

Sales of my art work is pretty steady. There are six galleries willing to show my work annually."

"Good for you. And how's Clara doing?"

"She's doing pretty well. You won't believe what she and her friend Penny did for me. Since she was never going back to her apartment, she decided to sell the two paintings I gave her and Bob. They were purchased at auction by the Carl Hammer Gallery for a total of $83,000!"

"Oh my goodness, that's amazing, Hunter!"

"She said she didn't need the money, so she gave me the check. Can you believe it?"

"Congratulations! Mr. Not-So-Starving Artist!"

"Thanks. And how are things going for you?"

"Really well, thanks. Set record sales for this year. Couldn't be better."

"I'm not surprised. You really know marketing."

"Thanks. And thanks for calling about Clara."

That evening Janet dressed for a night out. She was meeting a guy she met online. His profile indicated he was a doctor, perhaps older than she, and dropped hints that he was well off financially. She was so sick of younger men who were only interested in sex, or her money, or the security she seemed to offer.

She arrived a little before seven, at the agreed-upon Bar and Grill. She told the hostess she was waiting for a friend. Ron showed up precisely at seven o'clock. Open collar shirt under an expensive sweater and sport coat. At the bottom of his blue jeans, a pair of designer shoes.

"You must be Janet," he said sweetly.

"And you must be Ron," she replied. They made a little small talk until shown to their table. She learned he was an orthopedic surgeon.

"Can you believe I make $100 grand for each surgery? Of course that also has to cover my expenses."

"I'm impressed," was all Janet could reply.

"I'm hungry for the steak and lobster," he announced. "Feel free to order whatever you'd like."

"Fish and chips sounds good to me," she replied enthusiastically.

"Oh, c'mon. You can do better than that!"

"That's what I'm hungry for," she smiled. Janet was not impressed with Ron's efforts to impress. Why can't she find just a normal, nice guy? They chatted cordially throughout the dinner. She learned he was divorced for about a year and had two grown sons.

"Would you like to go somewhere else for a drink, or want to check out a movie?" he asked.

"No. I don't think so. I'm pretty tired. Think I'll just head home." As Janet left the restaurant she sighed to herself. He's got money. But recently divorced and trying way too hard to impress. I hope he finds his needy princess. No thanks, not me.

A month later she was with another online acquaintance. They had chatted for a couple of weeks and Chuck seemed to have possibilities. His communication showed him to be very interested in learning about her, her work, her family, her favorite foods, and activities, even her religious faith. They met for coffee on Saturday afternoon.

"You told me you like vanilla latte. Let me get that for you," Chuck offered.

"Thank you very much." Janet smiled. He remembered her favorite.

They sat down at a small table in the corner of the coffee shop. Janet began asking Chuck about his favorites.

"Straight mocha, the Lakers, the Padres, can't stand golf, it's too slow. Movies: Star Wars, Ocean's Eleven, Princess Bride. Charities: St. Jude's Children's Hospital, American Cancer Society, and local food bank."

"Wow! Sounds like you've been through that list before."

"A time or two. Now tell me, you mentioned that you moved here from Chicago. Have you made many new friends here?"

"Not really. Just my work acquaintances."

"Let me assure you, I'm here for you. You need anything, you call me, understand? Anything. Just give me a heads up."

The sound of his voice and the pathetic look of compassion made Janet want to scream. He is so paternalistic. Maybe he is a nice guy. Maybe he really would help if I needed him. No, he's just too much. I don't need to be taken care of.

After half an hour of "caring conversation," Janet excused herself. "I promised my friend I'd meet her and do some shopping this afternoon. It's her mother's birthday on Monday." A little white lie was better than trying to explain.

Janet decided to swear off the online matches for the time being. She focused on her work, taking care of the cat, and watering her plants. It was during her second summer in L.A. she became aware of how often her eyes were burning from the smog. She detested the traffic on the freeways. The palm trees were no longer a new image; she hardly noticed them anymore. The beauty was wearing off. Now that she could see beyond the glamour of Hollywood, Janet began to dread the smog, the pollution, and the traffic.

Evenings were the hardest. Sometimes she just sat staring at the TV until ten or so, then decided it was time for bed. It was becoming apparent she had fallen back into the old Chicago patterns of eat, work, sleep, and be depressed. Why depressed? Things were really going well at work. What was wrong? Nothing she could put her finger on. Then she remembered her brother. She called and learned that Trish had still not returned. Well, there's one thing that's wrong. But I'm fortunate. I'm good at what I do. I shouldn't be depressed. But I am. I hate to admit it, but I am.

CHAPTER TWENTY-THREE

YEAR TWO

"Hey Janet, I noticed you didn't seem too excited about the new television ads we're running."

"No, no, they're good. You and Jake and the film crew did a great job. I can't believe all the information you packed into 30 seconds."

"Thanks. Are you tired or something? You just haven't seemed yourself lately."

"Thanks Heather, yeah, I've been tired but I'm not sure why."

"Too much exercise or not enough?

Janet laughed. "Funny you should mention exercise. I'm sure I haven't been doing too much."

"Why don't you join me at the gym after work? You can come as my guest for a time or two."

"Hmm. That's not a bad idea. Maybe I will."

"I've got some extra sweat pants and shirts in my locker. You can borrow them."

"Sounds great. I'll use yours tonight and bring my own things for next week. See you after work."

For the next few weeks Janet worked out with Heather three evenings a week and an hour on Saturdays. It felt really good to be stretching and doing cardio workouts. When she came home she was exhausted and yet exhilarated. This is exactly what's been missing, physical exercise. After a one month trial, Janet paid for full membership. She was delighted to learn that her company insurance even paid for her hours at the gym, a part of the Wellness Program.

After a few months she stopped going on Saturdays. She met Heather on Mondays, Wednesdays. and Fridays after work. Heather was a fitness maniac. Weight lifting, aerobics, running laps, she pushed herself mercilessly and expected the same from Janet. Finally Janet told her she couldn't compete. "I admire your discipline, Heather, but I'll never be able to keep up with you. I think I'll just set my own pace and goals. I hope you don't mind."

"No, I don't mind. I just thought you needed the incentive."

"Well, I certainly did when I started. Thank you so much for getting me going here."

"You still okay with the three evenings a week after work?"

"Yeah, that works for me," Janet replied.

"See you Wednesday after work," Heather hit Janet teasingly on the shoulder and ran off to do her laps.

During the next few months Janet's depression returned. Again she asked herself, why? I thought the exercise was what I needed. Now I'm fit as can be. I'm successful as can be. But I come home, feed the cat, water the plants, watch TV, and wonder, why? Why am I working so hard? Am I afraid of failure? Should I look for a different job? Why am I depressed again?

One evening in the midst of her depression, she became aware that her phone was buzzing. It was on the coffee table in front of her, so she decided to pick it up. It was Hunter calling.

"Hello, Janet, this is Hunter."

"Hey Hunter!" she tried to sound excited to hear from him.

"I've got some exciting news and just had to call."

"What is it?" Janet wasn't excited but wanted to be happy for Hunter.

"I just opened the Hunter Gallery on West Division."

"Your own gallery? How magnificent!"

"Remember several months ago, I told you about the big check Clara Gerber gave me from the sale of my paintings?"

"Yes, that was a wonderful gift."

"Clara is still giving orders, and she wanted me to get my own gallery. It took me a while to do it but I used her check to rent a small store and get it renovated with lights and everything."

"I'm proud of you, Hunter. I'm proud that you were willing to take the risk of starting your own gallery."

"It would have been a lot easier if you were still here to help me get started."

"Well, thank you for your confidence. Sorry I couldn't be there."

"Next time you're in Chicago on business or in Milwaukee to see your parents you'll have to visit my gallery. It's small, but I think you'll like it."

"I'm sure I will. I definitely want to see it. And see you. And see your latest works."

"Thanks Janet. You know you're welcome any time."

"I'll probably fly back for Christmas. Maybe I can even talk my folks into coming to Chicago with me to see The Hunter Gallery of exceedingly fine art!"

Hunter laughed. "I hope you will. It would be nice to see them again."

"I never met your parents," Janet commented.

"And you probably never will!" Hunter joked.

"Thanks for calling. I'm really happy you have your own gallery. Keep me posted on how it goes."

"I will. G'night, Janet."

"Good night, Hunter." For the first time in months, Janet got ready for bed with happy thoughts and feelings. Nothing at all romantic. Just thinking about her old friends, and how she missed them. She remembered all the help she had given Hunter, and was soon sound asleep.

The following week Hunter called again. "Hey Janet. I forgot to tell you something else about my gallery."

"What did you forget?" Janet asked.

"Well, when I went to the Retirement Center to tell Clara the good news about the gallery, she had another crazy idea."

"Same old Clara. I just love her spirit. What was her crazy idea this time?"

"She said, just like she always does, 'Here's what we're going to do. You're going to come get me on Tuesdays and Thursdays, and I'm going to be the docent at your gallery those two days every week.'"

Janet burst out laughing. "That is so Clara! Is she well enough to do that?"

"She is pretty weak, but she said she could sit at the gallery as easily as she could sit in her room at the Center. So anyway, we tried it. And so far, it's working."

"Amazing, amazing."

"It is amazing. She's amazing! Anyway, the reason I'm calling tonight is she made her first sale at the gallery today. A young couple came in and loved one of my new paintings. She told me they were on vacation and loved to browse art galleries. She said they had a private conversation and then decided to buy the painting. She was so proud of herself for writing up the sale and giving them a receipt for their check. I just had to share the excitement with you."

"Thank you, Hunter. Thank you for calling. I sure miss you guys."

"Oh, and one more thing before I hang up," Hunter added. "I went to the doctor yesterday for another melanoma. This one was on my chest, just above my stomach."

"Oh not again. Did he remove it?"

"Yeah, he did. And he sent the tissue to the lab. I guess I won't hear anything until next week."

"Sure sorry to hear about that. You take care of yourself, and call me if you hear any further word from the doctor. And once again, thanks for taking care of Clara."

"She's no bother. In fact, sometimes it seems she's taking care of me."

Janet had to admit, she really did miss the meetings of the Hunter Art Corporation. She was happy that Hunter had opened his own gallery. She would definitely visit him on her next trip to the Midwest.

The following Christmas Janet booked her flight to Chicago. Her parents said if the weather was not too bad, they would meet her at O'Hare. She told them she wanted to see Hunter's gallery before heading home to Milwaukee. The flight arrived about noon, and the weather was good, so they drove to West Division to visit Hunter and see his gallery.

"Hi Janet, please come in," Hunter said as he held the door for Janet and her parents.

"Hunter, you remember my folks, Brad and Elise Sadler?"

"Yes, we met at the airport when you left Chicago. Please let me show you around the gallery."

"Oh my, Janet. You were right. Hunter has some beautiful paintings," her mom gushed.

"I like the ones with forest animals. I used to do a lot of hunting," her dad commented.

"Oh Dad, you never were much of a hunter. I don't think you ever shot anything."

"I did too. I shot a rabbit once."

Janet turned to Hunter. "How are things working out with Clara?" Janet asked. "Is she still coming to sit here during the week? I couldn't believe it when you told me how she insisted on working here."

"Yup, I'm still amazed. Twice a week. She can barely walk to get to the restroom, but she insists she wants to keep coming."

"I do wish we had time to see her. It gets dark early now, so we'd better get on the road. Please say hello to Clara next time you see her. And give her a big Christmas hug from me."

"I'll do that. She'll be so glad you came to see the gallery."

In a short time the tour was over and the Sadler's headed for Milwaukee. Hunter was about to turn out the lights when he noticed a note on his desk which hadn't been there before.

> The check under this note is for your painting
> of the two deer in the forest. I want to buy it
> for my folks for Christmas, for Dad especially.
> Please use the extra $50 for shipping it to their
> home, see address below. Fondly, Janet

Hunter shook his head in disbelief. He remembered how much he disliked her when they first began working together. She had signed the note with the word "fondly." An old saying came to mind, "Absence makes the heart grow fonder." It was true. He missed Janet.

CHAPTER TWENTY-FOUR

NOT SO HAPPY NEW YEAR

His phone was buzzing. Hunter hated to be interrupted when he was painting. Sometimes he just let it go to the answering service. He glanced to see if it was a robo-call or someone he knew. It was Janet.

"Hi Hunter. I just got off the phone talking with my parents. They are thrilled with your painting."

"Hi Janet. That's great. I'm glad they like it. How's the new year going for you?"

"Too soon to tell about January. We finished last year strong with record sales for December. I've just been catching up with things that didn't get done while I was at my folks'. How is your January going?"

"I've been spending more time at the gallery since the holiday. Clara came down with a bad cold right after Christmas."

"Oh, I'm sorry to hear that. Wish her well for me, will you?"

"Sure will. I'll keep you posted on her recovery."

Several evenings later Hunter called Janet. "I've got some bad news, Janet. They just sent Clara to the hospital with pneumonia."

"Oh no. How bad is she?"

"Hard to say. She's on oxygen and very weak. I was there this afternoon and I could barely get her to wake up."

"Oh, Hunter. This doesn't look good. I've heard that people her age don't have much of an immune system to fight infections like pneumonia."

"Yeah, but she's on IV antibiotics."

"I certainly hope they can pull her through. You keep me informed, okay?"

"Thanks Janet, I'll call if there's any change in her condition."

Hunter stopped at the hospital the next morning to check on Clara before opening the gallery.

"Hi Clara. You certainly look more alert than you were yesterday."

"Hi Hunter. Were you here yesterday?"

"Yes, but you were sleeping most of the time."

"I do that a lot lately," she said with a smile.

"How are you feeling?" Hunter asked.

"Pretty chipper! But the nurse told me, No dancing!" Clara laughed at her little joke.

"At least you've still got your sense of humor."

"When that's gone, I'm gone," Clara replied. "Now that I'm feeling better, see if you can take me to the gallery today. Would you ask the nurse?"

"Oh, I wish you could sit at the gallery. Maybe next week when you're a little stronger."

"Here's what we're going to do, Hunter," Clara began. Hunter chuckled wondering what crazy idea she would suggest this time. "Tonight, a little after ten o'clock, I want you to sneak into the hospital with my coat and a nice warm scarf. You'll wrap me up and we'll walk out of here like we were visiting some other patient. Got that?"

"Got it. I'd better get to the gallery; it's almost time to open up."

Hunter leaned over her bed to give her a hug. He whispered, "And I'll see you tonight, a little after ten."

Clara hung onto his arm for what seemed like a minute or more. Hunter finally pulled free and left the room. He was so glad she was getting better. The antibiotics must be working.

Hunter was eating breakfast and watching the morning news when his phone buzzed.

"No! No that can't be! She was fine yesterday." Hunter could feel the tears forming.

The phone call was from the Director of Nursing at the retirement home. "The call from the hospital came about 4 am according to the nurse's notes. I thought I'd wait until seven to call you. I hope I didn't wake you up."

"I was awake. So are you saying she passed away about 4 am?" Hunter asked.

"Yes, according to the notes I have here. I just spoke with Mrs. Gerber's friend, Penny, to inform her of Clara's passing. The funeral home Clara had designated has taken her to the mortuary for embalming. Here's their number."

Hunter sat silently for about fifteen minutes, his thoughts bringing periods of intermittent tears. Finally he roused himself and called Janet. She answered after the fourth ring. "Hello?"

"Janet, this is Hunter."

"I should have guessed. Who else would call me at five-thirty in the morning?"

"Oh my gosh, I forgot about the time difference. I'm so sorry. I wasn't thinking. I just got a call from the retirement center. They told me Clara passed away early this morning about 4 a.m. I knew you'd want to know."

"That's sad news to wake up to, but I'm not surprised."

"I was shocked," Hunter replied. "She seemed fine yesterday."

"But from what you told me a couple of days ago, I thought she might not make it."

"Yeah, but yesterday she sounded like her old self. Even telling me to come back after ten p.m. and sneak her out of the hospital. Doesn't that sound just like her?"

"Maybe she had a premonition she wasn't going to be in there much longer."

"Maybe," Hunter answered.

A memorial service was held the following Saturday. Penny made arrangements for a local pastor to preside at the Senior Center where she and Clara had enjoyed playing Bingo. About a dozen acquaintances from the Center attended, along with four staff members from the retirement center. Janet was not able to come from California so Hunter felt pretty much alone. He was glad to see the manager from his apartment building. During the luncheon that followed the service, his manager sat down at his table and told him several stories about the Gerbers that Hunter had never heard. Memories. Oh, the memories.

Sunday, the day after Clara's memorial, Hunter opened the gallery at noon. He sat down in Clara's chair by the window and began sobbing. There in the mid-day sun lay her knitting needles and yarn. He blamed himself for her death. *If I hadn't brought her here. If I hadn't exposed her to the cold winter air. Maybe I didn't have the heat up high enough in here. Maybe sitting here for that many hours was too much for her. I should have brought her here only one day a week instead of two.* He held her knitting to his face, smelled the memories, and he cried.

Hunter spent the entire day on Sunday thinking about Clara, then about Bob. He wouldn't be here in the Hunter Gallery if they hadn't taken charge that night he tripped on the stairs. The apartment building felt different now, with new neighbors in Janet's place and now the Gerber's. Several visitors came into the gallery that afternoon but they didn't buy anything. Shortly after five o'clock Hunter realized he hadn't eaten lunch and he was hungry. He put Clara's knitting into the bottom drawer of the desk, took one more look around the room, turned out the lights, locked the door, and took the next bus back to his apartment.

CHAPTER TWENTY-FIVE

THE GALLERY
WITHOUT CLARA

Without his friend Clara watching the gallery, Hunter wasn't sure he could manage. He laid around the apartment for a couple of days not accomplishing much of anything. He thought about cutting back the gallery hours. There had been very few visitors and even fewer sales during the week. He wanted to be home painting on Monday and Tuesday, so decided to post hours for Wed - Thurs, 10 am to 6 pm; Fri – Sat, noon to 8 pm; and Sundays, noon to 4 pm.

Wednesday morning he dragged himself out of bed, dressed, ate breakfast, and caught the bus to go open the gallery. He unlocked the door, turned the sign to open, walked back to the desk and sat down. After a few minutes his eyes dropped to the lower drawer and he remembered Clara's knitting. He looked around just to make sure no one was watching, pulled the drawer open, and picked up the needles and yarn. Why not? The stitch was familiar. Why not finish Clara's project? It took several tries to get his stitches as tight as Clara's but he finally got a good looking row added to her shawl. Finishing it in her memory would be fun.

Just before closing, Hunter heard the bell above the door ring. He pulled the desk drawer open, quickly dropped the knitting into the drawer and pushed it shut. The person who entered was his old friend Nathan.

"Hey, Nathan! What brings you to the Hunter Gallery?"

"Haven't been here since your grand opening," Nathan replied. "Just thought I'd drop by and see how things are going."

"Kinda slow right now. I'm really frustrated. I don't know if you heard, but my friend and neighbor, Clara Gerber, was sitting the gallery two days a week. She just passed away, so I've lost my help and I don't know how I'm going to cover all the days I'm open. You got any ideas?" Hunter asked.

"I hear ya. It does get frustrating sometimes," Nathan replied. "I've got a system that you might consider. Remember how I always had several artists' work on display?"

"Yeah, including mine," Hunter smiled.

"I still invite artists to show their work, but only on a monthly basis. One or two artists a month. And I require them to spend at least one day a week working, I call it volunteering, at the gallery."

"Hey, that's a cool idea."

"Not only does it save me from hiring someone, it also brings more customers into the gallery, friends of the artists who come to see their friend's art, but also see mine."

"Kind of a two-for-one."

"Exactly," Nathan grinned. "I had another thought the other day, so I went on line and googled Hunter Gallery. Nothing came up in Chicago, but there is a Hunter gallery in Santa Fe."

"Darn, I meant to update my website when I opened, but I never got around to it."

"You've got a website?" Nathan asked.

"Yeah, Janet helped me set it up before she moved to California, but it's really outdated."

"Have you done any social media?"

"Not recently," Hunter admitted. "Janet really encouraged me, but I've kinda lost interest."

"What do you do here when there aren't any customers?" Nathan asked.

Hunter hated to admit he knitted. "Oh, I read books from the library. And I've got a sketch pad I draw on sometimes."

"Get going, Hunter. You're not going to sell much if you don't build your community."

"That's what Janet always said," Hunter sighed.

"One more thing I wanted to suggest," Nathan offered. "Remember I mentioned a gallery in Santa Fe? Well, you might want to get to know their people. It's a really successful place. You might ask if they'd be interested in showing some 'Hunters' at their Hunter Squared Gallery. Be sure to tell them you've got two works at the Carl Hammer Gallery in Chicago."

"Isn't that a little pushy?" Hunter asked.

"Heck, if you don't push a little, you'll never get anywhere in this world. I always say, 'It's worth a try. Nothin' to lose.' Anyway, give it some thought. I gotta run."

"Thanks for dropping by. And thanks for some good ideas."

"Good luck Hunter. I've always liked your work." The bell rang again as Nathan left.

Hunter went to his desk and was about to pull out his knitting. He pushed the drawer shut and started making notes. Nathan's suggestions had real possibilities. *Tomorrow,* Hunter thought, *I've got to remember to bring my laptop here and get to work on the website and my social media. Maybe I will try to contact that gallery in New Mexico.*

CHAPTER TWENTY-SIX

THE CHICAGO PERIOD

T he following Monday morning Hunter ate breakfast but didn't feel like painting. He went out the door to get on the bus and remembered the gallery didn't need to be opened on Mondays. He got on the bus anyway, and after going past the gallery, transferred to another bus that took him to the Loop. Once downtown he walked to Michigan Avenue and thought about going into the Art Institute. He looked up the stairs at the entrance and decided to walk through Millennium Park instead. Before going any farther, he stopped at an art supply store and bought a sketch pad and several pencils. He sat in the Park and did a couple of sketches of the reflecting pool, people strolling by, and a nearby fountain. He tucked the pad under his arm and continued walking.

A short time later Hunter found himself at Navy Pier. He bought a ticket and climbed into the large, slow-moving ferris wheel that lifted him high above Lake Michigan, with a fabulous view of the Chicago skyline. He did a couple of quick sketches of the skyline and was soon back at the bottom of the ride. Strolling out

JIM BORNZIN

to the end of the pier he found a bench where he could enjoy the view and breezes off the lake. Oh, how he missed Clara. And Bob. And Janet.

Tuesday was also a day for painting. The gallery would remain closed until Wednesday. Hunter opened his new sketch pad and chose a scene for a new canvas. The Chicago skyline was a very rough sketch, and Hunter wasn't sure the buildings were accurately portrayed. *Accuracy be damned*, he said to himself. He wanted to capture the feelings of buildings rising up from the earth, the feeling of clouds and gulls soaring, maybe even soaring below the vantage point of the viewer. Tuesday evening Hunter was excited. His impressionist view was becoming a reality. Another day or two and it would be finished and ready for framing.

In the weeks and months that followed, Hunter fell into a new routine. Mondays became his sketch day somewhere in Chicago. For a couple of weeks he focused on the "L." He sat beneath the elevated tracks sketching street views. He climbed the stairs to the platform and sketched the trains as they roared by. He spent a day at the Museum of Science and Industry, walking, exploring, meditating, and sketching. Time and again he walked the lakeshore with pad in hand. He observed planes flying over the lake from the east, heading toward O'Hare Airport. He sketched the sailboats skimming over the waves.

On a beautiful fall day in October, he drove his car out from the city and parked in one of the many forest preserves that surround the city. The fall foliage inspired a number of works in the months that followed. In December he captured a scene focused on a railroad bridge covered in snow. He laughed when he saw a woman walking three dogs that wanted to go in different directions. So he sketched and painted an exaggerated version of the three dogs and tangled leashes.

Back in the gallery toward the end of each week, Hunter tried to update his website and post his new paintings on social media. Most months he was able to find another artist whose work was featured near the front of the gallery. And most guest artists were

108

willing to spend one day a week or a couple of weekends hosting the gallery so Hunter didn't have to be there. Nathan was right about featuring guest artists. It had given him more time to paint. They brought new visitors to the gallery. And it gave him a reason to update his website each month. Janet would be proud.

That Christmas Hunter called Janet and they talked for nearly an hour.

"You won't believe what I've been doing," Hunter began. "I've got a new thing I do on Mondays, and sometimes on Tuesdays, when I don't have to be at the gallery. I've been traveling around Chicago and sketching."

"That sounds like fun," Janet responded. "Where have you been?"

"The first month or so I went downtown, you know, Millennium Park, the lake front, Navy Pier, and the Loop. I spent a lot of time at the forest preserves this fall."

"And how are things at the Hunter Gallery?" Janet asked.

"Pretty good. At first, I was really lost without Clara."

"I find it hard to believe she's gone. She had such vitality."

"I really miss her. My friend Nathan suggested I invite a Guest Artist of the Month whose work is featured to draw more visitors. They have to volunteer to host the gallery one day during the week or on the weekend. That's really helped."

"Are you selling any paintings?" Janet asked.

"Oh, a few. Enough to pay the bills, you might say. And how's work going for you?"

"Pretty well. I've brought a lot of new ideas for marketing campaigns, and our sales are climbing. I really like my marketing team. My assistant, Karl Hesterman, is Manager of Online Marketing. He's always coming up with new ideas."

When the conversation was over, Hunter wished her continued success, and remembered how her enthusiasm had lifted his spirits years ago.

The following spring Hunter found himself at the Lincoln Park Zoo. He had always loved animals, but this year he was observing them in a new way. Sometimes he'd ask himself, *What would Clara say to this critter?* He was sure she would have good advice, something this animal needed to do to improve its situation. He looked for anything that made him chuckle. Then he would try to sketch it, or exaggerate the action in his drawing. By summer he had a dozen new animal paintings ready to display at the gallery. He also had a theme for his summer show, and good material for his website and social media.

He decided to call this past year his "Chicago period" and to dedicate these works to Bob and Clara Gerber. He could still hear Clara telling him, *Hunter, here's what we're going to do. On Sunday nights, you'll sit down with me and Bob and report on your work. I want a full report with two parts. Part One, your sketching and painting. Part Two, your marketing and business report on the gallery.* So that's what he did. Most Sunday evenings he would come back from the gallery, or take a break from painting. He would sit down in the kitchen with a sandwich and a beer. On his laptop he'd write his weekly report, pretending he was talking with Bob and Clara. Oh, how he missed them.

CHAPTER TWENTY-SEVEN

I NEED YOU TO ...
DO SOMETHING FOR ME

Janet, too, was grieving. She had grieved leaving Chicago, her parents, her friends at work, and Hunter. But she missed the Gerbers most of all. Living in California she felt like she could go back and see them anytime. Now it was certain she could not. Bob had died a few years ago, and now Clara. They were both gone. Janet slipped back into bouts of depression.

Her late afternoon or early evening trips to the gym helped shorten the evening hours after work. Weekends were the worst. Sometimes she worked on marketing projects on her PC at home. Once the work was caught up, she went crazy with nothing to do. Sometimes she even missed Hunter. She never thought that would happen.

Things were going well at her job, but her boss, the Western Region President, had an annoying habit. Instead of asking her to promote a certain product with a question: Janet, would you?

Or with a command: Janet, I'd like you to. He always phrased his directions: Janet, I need you to. I need you to change the January sales items. I need you to get more photographs. Why does he need me to? Can't he do anything himself? Why can't he just say Please?

The spring sales events had just wrapped up when the President came into her office. "Janet, I know you thought Mary was going to work out if we gave her enough time, but we don't have time for on-the-job training. I've made my decision. I need you to tell Mary she's being let go." Without any further explanation, he turned and walked out the door.

Janet wanted to scream, but didn't. She wanted to cry, but didn't. HE made the decision. Why doesn't HE tell Mary? She walked to Mary's desk and asked if she would come to her office. There, she told Mary, as delicately and compassionately as she could that Mary's position was being terminated. Mary began to cry. Janet pulled Kleenex from the box and handed them to Mary. "This wasn't my decision," Janet explained. "The company is looking for ways to cut costs. Cutting positions is one way to do that."

"But you just hired me six months ago," Mary whined.

"I know. And I'm sorry." There was really nothing more Janet could tell her.

After work Janet went to the gym and got rid of some of her frustration. She picked up her favorite shrimp salad on the way home. As she came in the door her phone rang.

"Hi, Dad," she answered.

"Hi Janet. I've got to keep this short. Your mom's in the other room and I don't want her to hear me talking to you."

"Okay. I'm listening."

"You know how much your mom loves the California dates your brother used to send. He hasn't sent any for the past year or two. Well, Easter is coming, and I need you to buy some of those dates and have them sent to me so I can give them to Mom."

Janet knew her brother was having trouble managing his own life and wasn't thinking much of others. She wondered why her dad couldn't go online to order the dates. Well, he's not very savvy and probably doesn't know how to do that. Maybe he does "need me to."

"Sure, Dad. I'll take care of it."

"Thanks, honey. Don't say anything to Mom," he whispered. "G'bye."

Janet swore she would never use that phrase, ever! Everyone needs me to do something. I should just be glad I'm so capable and so reliable. She sat down in the kitchen to eat her salad. The phone rang again.

"Hello."

"Hi Janet. It's Ralph."

"Hey Ralph, I was just thinking about you. How are things going with you and Trish?"

"Well, that's why I'm calling. Have you got a minute?"

"Sure, what's up?"

"We were in court today. Trish filed for divorce. She also got custody of the kids."

"Oh, Ralph. I'm so sorry to hear that."

"She also got the house. So I've got one week to pack my stuff and get out."

"Oh, what a bummer."

"So what I was wondering is … would you mind if I came to live at your place for a month or two?"

Janet couldn't believe it. "What about your job?" she asked.

"Well, I've been so depressed for so long I really need to find something new."

Janet closed her eyes and wished this wasn't happening. "Can't you find a job in San Jose?"

"I don't want to stay in San Jose. I need someplace to recover from this mess. I need a fresh start. I need you to say I can come live with you."

After a long silence Janet replied. "Of course, Ralph. You're my brother. You're welcome to stay with me as long as you need."

"Oh Janet, I knew I could count on you. I won't stay any longer than necessary. That I can promise."

"I'll get a bedroom ready for you. When will you come?"

"Friday is my last day at work. I'll drive down on Saturday."

Janet hung up the phone and finished her shrimp salad. She was angry. She was depressed. She watched television for about an hour. "Janet," she said to herself, "I need you to get ready for bed."

CHAPTER TWENTY-EIGHT

KEEPING YOUR BALANCE

The next afternoon at the gym, Janet and Heather were in the locker room at the same time. Heather seemed bouncy and full of energy, even after a strenuous workout.

"How do you do it?" Janet asked.

"Do what?" Heather smiled in reply.

"How can you be so energetic after a full workout?"

"I wouldn't say I feel energetic. But I am excited."

"Excited about what?" Janet asked.

"Well, tonight our church youth group is meeting at the Gospel Mission to serve meals."

"Aren't you a little old to be in a youth group?" joked Janet.

"No, silly, I'm one of the adult sponsors. I love working with the kids."

"What church is that?"

"Evangelical Church in Christ." Heather answered. "Do you go to church?"

JIM BORNZIN

"No, not since I was just a little kid and my parents made me go to Sunday School."

"You ought to try it. Maybe you'll make some new friends," Heather suggested.

"Maybe I will," Janet replied as she tied her shoes.

"You're welcome to come to my church," Heather offered.

"Thanks, but I'll have to think about it."

"Have a good night!" Heather hollered as she went out the door.

At home that evening Janet reflected on Heather's suggestion. Maybe going to church would help my depression. It would be nice to meet some new friends, someone I don't work with. Ralph will be here next week. Maybe he'll need to go to church. At least it would give me something to do on Sunday mornings, one of the times I've had so much trouble getting out of bed. After doing some online research, Janet decided to try Holy Trinity Lutheran Church in Inglewood, a short drive from home. Before turning off her computer, she did another search, looking for California dates. She ordered a box and had it sent to her dad.

The following Sunday morning was sunny and warm. Janet drove to Holy Trinity and liked the Spanish style architecture of the church. The people inside welcomed her as she made her way into the sanctuary. She enjoyed singing the opening hymn and she appreciated the confessional prayer. The pastor's sermon was not judgmental, and spoke of joy and hope.

"Eternal life floods the soul in moments when we know the extraordinary love of Christ within. All doubt and fear evaporate. Hatred and anger are gone. Fear flees. Sadness and feelings of inferiority or self-importance disappear. All that remains is the total assurance of this love, telling us that all is and will be well. The moment may last ever so briefly, but in that moment we have tasted eternity, and we know that nothing else matters even half so much as knowing this love." *Pastor David L. Miller, St. Timothy Lutheran Church, Naperville, IL, from *Christ in Our Home*, November 28, 2019

Janet's soul was touched in that moment. She could see and

116

hear Bob and Clara smiling and talking to her, reassuring her of their love and God's.

The pastor continued, "We cannot give ourselves this joy and hope. It comes as a gift Christ is pleased to give as we draw near and feast on his words, as we open our hands to receive the sacrament of his body and blood, and as we pray knowing our hearts are heard."

Janet couldn't remember if she had ever been baptized, but she made up her mind, she would walk forward to receive the sacrament of Christ.

Joy and hope are gifts. No matter how hard I work or how successful I am, I can't earn joy and hope. They are gifts from Christ. And they have been missing from my life.

The pastor concluded his sermon. "Seek the food that gives eternal life, every day. Set aside time to listen to Jesus. Imagine him as he speaks and walks among his disciples. Watch him as he reaches out in compassion to touch the broken. Do not let the busyness of life distract you from knowing him. For this is what your heart most needs." *David L. Miller

That afternoon Janet baked two trays of lemon muffins. When they had cooled slightly she put a dozen into a plastic bag and carried them across the street to her elderly neighbors' house. She rang the bell. "Hi, my name is Janet. I'm your neighbor across the street. I just finished baking these lemon muffins and thought you might enjoy them."

"Thank you," the gray-haired woman replied. "Plese come in?"

"No, no. Not this time. I just wanted to introduce myself. Maybe another time."

"Oh, you're so sweet. Thank you very much Janet."

Janet turned, and was gone. Walking back to her own house, she thought of Clara who had brought fresh baked goods to her apartment in Chicago. "Do not let the busyness of life distract you from knowing him. For this is what your heart most needs." The pastor's words were true, so true.

The second bag of muffins she took next door. The woman living there appeared to be single or divorced with two teenage sons. From the look of her car, and run-down appearance of the house, Janet assumed the woman was struggling financially. She rang the bell. A teenager answered.

"Hi, I'm Janet, your next-door neighbor."

"Hey, Mom!" the boy hollered, "It's for you!"

In a few moments the mother appeared. "How may I help you?" she asked.

"I just finished baking these lemon muffins and hoped you or your boys would like them," Janet replied as she handed the bag through the screen door.

"Well, thank you. I'm sure the boys will gobble them up in no time."

"Be sure to save one or two for yourself. If you like them, I'll do this again."

"That's very nice of you. My name is Maria. What is your name?"

"I'm Janet, and I live next door," Janet said pointing to her house.

"Thank you, thank you very much. I hope we can become friends."

"That would be wonderful," Janet replied. She stepped down off the porch and walked home. Her mind was reeling. Her physical self was working out at the gym. Her mental self was certainly being challenged at work. Now she could add the spiritual component which had been missing. *If I can just keep these three in balance, my emotional self should be getting better.* Back in her own home she drew a circle on a blank sheet of paper, then divided the circle in quarters: Mental, Physical, Emotional, and Spiritual. *All four are important. It seems so clear. But I've been so out-of-balance. No wonder I've been depressed. Attending church has got to be as good for me as the gym. Yes!*

Janet spent the rest of Sunday dragging the desk from her study into a corner of the living room, re-booting her computer, emptying the dresser, moving her extra clothes out of the closet, getting the room ready for her brother.

CHAPTER TWENTY-NINE

RALPH MOVES IN

The following Saturday Ralph pulled into the driveway at 4:15. Janet helped bring a few items into the house and showed him his room. "You can put your clothes in the closet, and the dresser is empty too." Janet did her best to welcome her brother. He looked tired, drained. "There's only one bathroom, so I guess we'll have to share it like we did when we were kids."

Ralph hauled in box after box plus several suitcases full of clothes. Everything was stacked in the bedroom that had been her office. There was barely room to walk around the bed.

"I can't thank you enough, Sis. I don't know how I'll ever repay you."

"Your thanks is all I need. I know you'd do the same for me." Janet had learned those nice phrases long ago. They came in handy when you didn't know what else to say. But saying them to her brother helped her express a love she wasn't feeling at the moment.

"I've got my laptop," Ralph said as he pulled it from one of the suitcases. "So I won't need to use your PC. Do you have a TV tray or something I could put it on?"

Janet brought a tray from the dining room. She looked around the bedroom. There was no place to set up the TV tray. "You can work on the dining room table if you want to. I don't use it very often. You and I will probably eat at the kitchen counter."

"Oh, that would be great. I'll get started on my job search on Monday." Ralph took the laptop to the dining room then started putting clothes away.

"I'll go fix a little supper," Janet said. "Holler if you need anything."

"Janet!" he said sharply, stopping her in her tracks. "I can't thank you enough."

In the days that followed Ralph spent most of the day online looking for job postings. He worked on his résumé, and filled out job applications. Janet continued her workouts at the gym and invited Ralph to come as her guest, but he declined. She was pleased when he had dinner prepared when she came home. Sometimes it was just a frozen dinner baked in the oven. Sometimes he prepared something from scratch. And sometimes they went out to eat.

By the second weekend, he was into his routine, and Janet was getting used to his being there. Saturday evening she asked him, "Ralph, would you like to go to church with me tomorrow?"

"I don't know." Ralph shrugged. "Depends. What kind of church is it?"

"Lutheran," Janet replied. "Kind of like Methodist or Episcopal."

"Not holy, holy super Christians?"

"No, nothing like that. What gave you that idea?"

"I just don't want anything to do with, I don't know, conversion-type evangelicals, like those evangelist preachers you see on TV. Trish went to a church like that, but I refused to go."

"I didn't know Trish was a church-going Christian," Janet said.

"Oh, you better believe it. So self-righteous. I guess that's one reason we didn't get along. I felt like I'd never be perfect enough for her."

"That must have been hard."

"It's hard to explain. She tried hard to be a perfect wife and mother. But she always let me and the kids know when we weren't pleasing the Lord."

"You don't have to go with me if you don't want to. I've just found the people to be very friendly, and the pastor's really nice. He talks mostly about grace and love, and compassion and kindness, stuff like that."

"Well, okay. I'll give it a try. What time do we leave for church?"

"Church starts at ten so I usually leave at 9:30," Janet answered.

"I'll set my alarm for 8:30 and see you in the morning."

CHAPTER THIRTY

HELPING OTHERS
HELPS JANET

After church on Sunday Janet and her brother, Ralph, stopped at a restaurant to eat.

"Well, what did you think?" Janet asked.

"I liked it. Nice church, and like you said, the people are friendly."

"What did you think of the pastor's sermon?"

"It was good. As he talked about Jesus interacting with the disciples, it felt real. Jesus seemed like a real guy, not some mythical divine being disguised as a human."

Janet laughed. "I agree. I heard one member say Lutherans have a down-to-earth faith."

"That's another way to put it," Ralph agreed.

Back at the house, Ralph wanted to check his emails, and go over his résumé once more. He was excited about an in-person job interview scheduled for Wednesday. Janet had just changed into casual clothes when she heard the doorbell. "I'll get it," she hollered from the bedroom.

Janet opened the door to see her next-door neighbor, Maria.

"Hello, señora. I have something for you." Maria held up a bag.

"Did you bake muffins?" Janet asked.

"No, señora, these are chimichangas. My boys love them, and I hope you like them too."

"Why thank you, Maria. How nice of you." Janet accepted the bag which felt warm on the bottom. "Would you like to come in?"

"Oh no. No thank you. You just enjoy." Maria turned and left.

"Who was that?" Ralph asked.

"My next-door neighbor, Maria," Janet answered. "C'mon in the kitchen and try one of these." Janet and Ralph munched on the chimichangas, oowing and aaahing at how good they tasted. "Last Sunday I took some muffins to her door, just to get acquainted," Janet explained. "But I think we got the better end of the deal."

"These sure are tasty. Mm-hmm," Ralph said as he reached for another.

Janet was surprised to find the months flying by as her brother continued his job search. Instead of being angry and depressed, she actually found herself enjoying her brother's company. They went to movies together, and continued their attendance at church. She continued to push him to come to the gym, or at the very least, to develop a workout routine at home. Ralph tried a few times, but the best he could do was a walk through the neighborhood most evenings after dinner.

Janet returned home from work and the gym one evening to find Ralph in the kitchen preparing dinner. She wasn't surprised until she walked through the dining room and saw the table set with her best china, candles, and wine goblets.

Turning back to the kitchen she grinned at her brother, "What's the occasion?"

"Would you believe, I got a job?" he smiled back.

"Really? Is it the one where you were one of three final candidates? You seemed pretty excited about getting that one."

"That's the one. I start the first of the month."

"Oh, Ralph, I'm really excited for you." She reached out and gave him a big hug.

"Would you mind if I stay here," Ralph asked, "for just another month or two to save up some money for rent?"

"No, not at all. Stay as long as you want," Janet replied.

"Aw, Sis, you're the greatest!"

Two months passed and again Janet came home to find the dining room table set for a formal dinner. "Okay, Ralph, what are we celebrating tonight?"

"I found an apartment, paid my first and last month's rent, and I'll be moving out this weekend," he said, "so we're celebrating!"

"I guess this means this is the last time you'll be fixing my dinner?"

"Well, I guess so. But maybe I'll invite you to my place for dinner. How would you like that?"

"I'd love it!" Janet hugged her brother. "Give me a few minutes to freshen up and change clothes."

"Sure, take as much time as you need. The roast is simmering in the crock pot."

"Mmmm, it smells good. Be right back."

It had been nearly six months since Ralph had moved in with her. Now it seemed like only six weeks. It had all turned out much better than she had expected. As sister and brother, they were closer now than they had been since grade school. Ralph's gratitude was deep and genuine. Janet reflected on the message she was hearing at church. God has a wonderful purpose for every life. She had not been depressed at all these past six months. Helping her brother had truly been a godsend.

CHAPTER THIRTY-ONE

PAINTING IN THE GALLERY

Hunter was excited about the marketing ideas Nathan had given him. For the next month or two he arrived at the gallery promptly at 10 am on Wednesdays and Thursdays, and at noon Friday through Sunday. He brought his laptop with him every morning and worked hard to get his website updated with new paintings and prices. He added photos of the gallery along with the hours it was open. He posted a few comments about the gallery and his new paintings on Facebook and Twitter. Then he picked up his sketchpad and began to draw. It was soon full of new ideas for paintings. He wished he had more time to start the new works that were coming alive in his mind.

One morning as he left the apartment, he grabbed a small blank canvas along with his laptop. He stuffed a handful of brushes and tubes of acrylics into his jacket pockets and headed out the door. At the gallery he opened the sketchbook and started copying one of his ideas onto the canvas. The pencil drawing got his juices flowing. He could hardly wait to get the acrylics open.

There were only two interruptions. He took a half hour break for lunch. And a potential customer walked in about 4:30, browsed through the gallery, complimented Hunter on his work, and left. Hunter resumed his painting. It was 6:15 when Hunter glanced at the clock. Where had the time gone? He usually watched the minutes tick by from 5:30 on, sometimes closing at 5:45. Today it had slipped past 6 pm, time to close up and get some dinner. He looked at the small canvas and smiled. He thought about taking it back to the apartment to finish, then realized it might be good to leave it here and finish it tomorrow. He had other paintings to work on at home.

For the next several months, Hunter took canvas after canvas to the gallery. He was excited when a customer would occasionally spend ten or fifteen minutes watching him paint. As he finished the small paintings, he would get them framed at a nearby frame shop, and then hang them in the gallery. He also brought finished paintings from his apartment and hung them as well. Finally, he added more lights to the bars on the ceiling, aiming them higher and lower at all his newer works.

Hunter didn't realize, until nearly a year had passed, that his sales were declining, while his website sat neglected and social media replies and comments went unanswered. All the good intentions from Nathan's suggestions had faded away. Hunter got lost in his painting. He had learned a lot, but couldn't overcome his singular desire to paint.

One of Nathan's ideas had turned into a real blessing. Hunter was inviting other artists to display their work, provided they would commit to hosting the gallery for one week, or five days during the month of their show. Hunter appreciated a much needed break from sitting at the gallery.

Several years passed with sporadic efforts at marketing. He corresponded with the Hunter Squared Gallery in New Mexico and was invited to send six of his best works there for a three month exhibit. Four of them sold and two were returned. It helped pay the rent for his little gallery in Chicago. Some years were financially better than others. One year was so dismal Hunter seriously considered closing the gallery. Hunter loved to paint. He loved giving birth to his colorful children which brought him such great joy! He still didn't like marketing.

CHAPTER THIRTY-TWO

JANET'S SUCCESS CONTINUES

T he years were flying and Janet had found a rhythm that was working. She was thriving with a well-balanced life of work and play, exercise and rest, and a faith that was active in worship and serving others. The salary increases she had earned at work verified the patterns of her life.

"Hello, Janet, this is Maria. May I come over to your house? I have something to show you."

"Certainly. You're welcome anytime."

In a few minutes Maria appeared at Janet's door with a flat box in hand. Janet greeted her at the door. "Come in, Maria. What do you have there?"

"I am so proud of this." Maria opened the box and lifted out her son's diploma. "Yesterday was my son's graduation from high school. He wore a cap and gown, and he looked so handsome! Look at this!" She handed the diploma to Janet.

"My, oh my. This is beautiful! And look at that gold seal at the bottom!"

"And Ricardo's name in that fancy lettering!"

"I can see why you are so proud," Janet commented and handed the diploma back.

"He will be going to the community college to study business. I hope he can be a big success like you!" Maria said excitedly.

"Why thank you, Maria. You tell Ricardo he *will be* a success if he studies hard and works hard. I guarantee it."

"Thank you, thank you. I will tell him." Maria turned and was gone.

Janet was also enjoying an occasional dinner with her brother. Sometimes they ate at his home, sometimes at Janet's. On his birthday, Janet took him to his favorite restaurant.

"Can you believe I'm turning 55?" Ralph asked as they were seated.

"Well, I'm not far behind," Janet replied. "It's hard to believe you've been here in Los Angeles fifteen years already."

"The time really has flown. How are things at work?" Ralph asked.

"Going really well. I'm in line for another promotion. Our Regional Vice-President will be retiring next year. I'll probably get the position, unless they bring in someone from the outside."

"I'm really proud of you, Sis. Even if you don't get it."

"Thanks. By the way, are you still meeting people online?"

"Naa. I gave that up a couple of years ago. How about you?" Ralph asked.

"Same for me. I just couldn't stand the guys I was meeting. My life's been less stressful without the dating scene."

"How 'bout that guy in Chicago you used to talk about?"

"Oh, you mean Hunter? I never dated him, just helped sell his paintings. I haven't heard from him in several years."

"You still going to that Lutheran church you took me to?"

"Yes I am. And would you believe, I'm even serving on the church council."

Ralph shook his head. "I never thought of you as the religious type."

"There's a big difference between religion and faith."

"What do you mean?" Ralph asked with a bewildered look.

"Well, religion is the formal expression of one's faith. Religion usually refers to practices and institutions. Faith is the personal, even private, relationship one has with God."

"Hmm. I never thought of it that way."

"My faith helps keep me in balance. I found I need to nurture my whole being: physical, mental, emotional, and spiritual."

"Wow! Well, it seems to be working. Your success is something I really admire."

As they finished their meal Janet reflected on Ralph's compliment. She was successful, and proud of her achievements. But she didn't want to tell Ralph about her lingering bouts with depression. They were fewer, and less intense than they used to be. She found that intensifying her workouts at the gym seemed to help get through her low periods. And focusing more fully on prayers of gratitude also helped.

A few evenings later her phone rang. It was Hunter.

"Hi Janet. How are you?"

"Doing well, Hunter. Thanks for calling. It's been a long time."

"Yes, I probably should call more often."

"No, that's okay. You're busy. I'm busy."

"You still climbing the corporate ladder?" Hunter asked.

"I'm still hanging on the corporate ladder. Not sure I'm climbing," Janet laughed.

Hunter chuckled in response. "Well, I'm calling 'cause I'm scared and don't know who else to talk to."

"Oh, Hunter, what's the matter?"

"Remember, quite a few years ago, I had a melanoma removed from my back?"

"Yes, I remember. That was around the time that old man Gerber died, wasn't it?"

"Well, it's back again."

"Hunter, I'm so sorry to hear that."

"Several spots on my back and groin. And this time the doctor said he wasn't sure he got it all."

"Oh, Hunter," was all she could say.

"How about you, Janet? How are you doing?"

"Had a bad time with my knee last year, but physical therapy helped me get back to the gym. I've been going pretty regularly."

"I should probably be getting more exercise," Hunter admitted.

"How are things at the gallery?"

"To be honest? Not so good." Hunter paused. "I could really use some help."

"Anything specific? Help with what?"

"I still don't like marketing."

"You probably never will. But as Clara used to say, 'Sometimes you have to do things you don't enjoy.'"

"I know, I know. I just wish you were here to help get me going."

"Hunter, old friend, sometimes I wish I could be there too. Partly because I need to get away from work here. And partly because I *almost* enjoyed working with you. Almost."

Hunter laughed. "And I almost enjoyed working with you."

"I'll say some prayers for you. You call again in a week or two and let me know what's happening, okay?"

"Okay. Thanks, Janet. Oh, and before I forget, I wanted to ask if you'd like another one of my paintings?"

"Well, of course, Hunter. I love your paintings. I'm not sure I can afford one now that you're so famous."

"I meant as a gift. I'd like to send you one. You don't have to pay me."

"I'd be delighted and honored. Did you have one in mind?"

"Yeah, it's from my Chicago period. Remember the year I spent doing scenes from around Chicago? Well there's one in particular from the park in our old neighborhood. I thought it might bring back some memories for you."

"Oh, Hunter, how sweet. Yes, I'd love it. I'm sure I'd just love it."

Janet promised herself she would definitely see Hunter the next time she was in Chicago. A week later a large box arrived

UPS. It was Hunter's painting. The old park looked familiar. There was the big maple tree where she used to spread her blanket for a picnic. There were kids on swings, mouths wide open with joy and laughter. The painting made her smile. It was one of Hunter's happy paintings, and it certainly did bring back memories from many years ago. She called Hunter to express her appreciation. There was no news about Hunter's cancer.

Two more weeks went by and Janet was again immersed in her work and deadlines. She had nearly forgotten her request that Hunter call her again. There was a message on her answering machine. Hunter had called while she was at the gym. She was about to call back when she remembered it was two hours later in Chicago. Better wait until tomorrow. The next day she forgot to call back. Hunter called again on Saturday.

"Hey Janet. Good news. The doctor injected a dye and did a biopsy of my lymph nodes and the cancer has not spread there."

"That is good news. So does that mean you are cancer free?"

"Not exactly. They said it was stage II; the worst is stage IV. I have to get checked every six months. I think it'll probably come back again."

"I'm sorry to hear that, Hunter."

"Well, at least I can breathe easy for the next six months. He said if the cancer does spread, the next step would be a surgery to remove the affected nodes."

"I certainly hope that won't be necessary."

"Me too."

The year drew to a close with Christmas and New Year's Eve. Janet was glad to have her brother nearby so they could celebrate these days together. She called her parents on Christmas Day and promised she would come home to Milwaukee in the coming year. Ralph was doing well in his job, already in his fifteenth year.

At Janet's office that spring everyone was wishing their boss a happy retirement. Janet was happy for him and though she couldn't tell anyone, she secretly wished she could retire as well. The announcement came shortly after the retirement party. The president of the corporation called from headquarters in Chicago. The Board of Directors had approved his recommendation to promote Janet to Vice-President of the Western Region. The board room in L.A. erupted with applause. Janet was moved with appreciation, joy, gratitude, and a deep sense of humility. A very nasty little voice whispered inside her head, *"So what?"*

CHAPTER THIRTY-THREE

HUNTER'S NEW ART FORM

Hunter sat at his kitchen counter and gazed around the apartment. It looked the same as it did twenty years ago. On the walls his better paintings hung. They were framed and ready to be taken to the gallery. But the gallery was full. There was no space for them there. Numerous paintings lined the room, stacked against the walls. He was proud of his early works, some still resided in the apartment and some were at the gallery. He almost hoped they wouldn't sell. He was proud of his "Chicago period," scenes from around the city. He was proud of his "dream works," which had been inspired by dreams or just ideas that came to him at night. But there was a new demon in his life that was beginning to affect his dreams. It was called "melanoma."

The gallery was moderately successful, at least bringing in enough income to pay his rent for both the apartment and the gallery. Some months he was short on grocery money, but he survived. He just spent more time at the easel instead of eating. Featured artists were scheduled on a regular basis throughout the year to keep the gallery's hours consistent. And Hunter didn't mind being there, as long as he could paint.

Hunter's favorite style of painting had always been realism, sometimes bordering on impressionistic, especially during his Chicago period. Some of his dream works were also more impressionistic than realistic, with bright splashes of color and light. Recently, however, his palette grew darker. He tried to tell himself not to worry about cancer. But his subconscious would not obey. He had trouble falling asleep, and then he'd dream. One night, after one particularly disturbing dream, he rose from the bed, slipped on his pants and shirt and went to the living room to paint.

He lifted a new canvas to the easel. He spread acrylics on his palette and washed a light gray onto the canvas. Next, he washed a darker gray onto the wet canvas with competing diagonal brushstrokes. Blotches of pink and orange and brown came next, some blotches touched with smaller spots of dark red. Morning light was glowing outside his window when he put finishing touches on his nightmare. Hunter was exhausted. He had been painting for nearly four hours. He lay down on his bed, still in his pants and shirt, and tried to get the images out of his mind. In a few minutes he was asleep. Then he heard his cell phone buzzing, 9 am, time to get up. Now full sun shone through the window.

Normally he was up by 8 without an alarm. He dragged himself into the bathroom and cleaned up for the day. Next he changed clothes, ate a bowl of Cheerios, and left to catch the bus. After a short ride he stepped down from the door of the bus and walked the short distance to the gallery. Hunter looked up at the sign, thinking it needed a fresh coat of paint. It looked so bright and fresh twenty years ago. He could hardly believe it had been that long since he hung that sign, since Clara had died. Twenty-two years since Janet had left for California.

Inside the gallery he turned on the lights and stared at his collection of art. Pretty amazing. It covered every wall, except the front section where the visiting artist had works displayed.

Hunter realized the guest artist had carefully chosen the location and spacing around each piece. It told the viewer each painting was special and deserved a space of its own. He glanced back at his own works, filling every wall, nearly floor to ceiling. How cluttered it appeared.

Hunter spent the rest of the day taking down his paintings. Slowly, wall by wall, one by one, he rearranged them. Well . . . half of them . . . placing them back on display. Each spot light was carefully repositioned. The pieces he had not restored to a place on the wall were placed behind the desk and file cabinet. Finally, half an hour before closing, Hunter strolled around the gallery evaluating his work. It had been a day well spent.

The next day was Friday. Before returning to the gallery at noon Hunter finished one of the acrylics he had been working on intermittently since his Chicago period. It was an expansive scene of Lake Michigan showing a sailboat in a strong wind. The sailor was leaning over the stern, hanging onto the rigging and reaching toward the water. Just beyond his outstretched hand, his hat floated over the crest of a wave! He wanted to take the painting with him to the gallery, but changed his mind. He wanted to be certain the acrylics had dried before carrying it on the bus. He had the perfect space in mind to show it.

On Saturday he realized he had not done any dreaded marketing for a long time. He pulled up the website and realized his last post was nearly a month ago. Hunter pulled out his phone and started taking pictures. First, his guest artist's work. That should be the feature of his new blog. Next, his own works. Man, they looked good with the new spacing and lighting! He began uploading the photos and writing about the featured artist. Janet would be proud. That evening several walk-ins commented on the blog and how it was the reason they had dropped in. He sold one of his paintings, and an hour later one of his friend's.

Hunter looked at the clock before closing. Two hours earlier in California. He called Janet and shared his excitement about rearranging his paintings, posting them on the website, and selling two works this evening. That night he fell asleep quickly. Sometime after midnight Hunter had another nightmare. He could see blobs of color slowly growing and expanding, growing and expanding. He awoke in a sweat, swore he would not try to paint this horrible vision, and finally fell back to sleep.

Several days later, killing time at the gallery, Hunter started a new canvas based on one of his dreams. Sinewy lines of red swarmed over a yellow and orange textured background. It was the most abstract thing he had ever painted. He wasn't sure he liked it. But the next day he decided to hang it. With the spot light shining brightly on it Hunter laughed to himself. It makes absolutely no sense. He gave it a ridiculous title: Mia La Noma. Reminds me of something I'd see in a New York gallery! Hunter thought New York artists were snobs. The day after that, someone bought it.

CHAPTER THIRTY-FOUR

BACK TO THE DOCTOR

H e was dreading this appointment. Six months after his node biopsy. The procedure had gone well, and there were no new signs of melanoma that Hunter could detect. The others in the waiting room were all older than he. He picked up a magazine from the stack on the table and immediately the nurse called him back to the examining room. He laid the magazine down and followed her down the hall.

The doctor was pleasant as he asked how Hunter was feeling.

"Pretty good, Doc. I haven't seen any new spots."

"That's a good sign. Here's the gown. You strip down and I'll be back in a few minutes."

When the doctor returned he began the full body exam. It made Hunter uncomfortable, but he knew it had to be done.

"Sorry to have to do this again. You remember the routine with the dye?" the doctor asked.

"Oh yeah, I remember," Hunter replied.

"After this injection, we'll check the nearby nodes to see if the cancer has spread there. If necessary, we'll do a localized surgery to remove those nodes. Do you have any questions?"

"No, I don't think so." Hunter was wondering *Am I gonna die?* but said nothing.

As if to confirm Hunter's worst fear, the dye did appear in a couple of the nodes. The procedure to remove them was done under local anesthetic, and left Hunter quite sore. Check back in a month. Have stitches removed. Six months later come back for another exam. Hunter decided not to call Janet this time. There was nothing new, really. Just the same old worry and anxiety.

Month by month Hunter checked his skin. No new spots appeared. But he was becoming more and more scared. The horrible dreams continued. Not every night, but at least once a week. He had always found painting a great escape, but it wasn't helping with his anxiety. He wasn't updating his social media or his website. He wasn't excited about painting. He didn't want to admit it, even to himself, but more and more hours at the gallery were spent . . . knitting.

The bell rang above the door. He dropped the knitting into the desk drawer and looked up. Is that Janet? Jumping from his chair he hollered, "Janet?"

"The one and only!" she hollered back.

Hunter ran to the front of the gallery and gave her a hug. "So great to see you!"

"You too, Hunter," she replied pulling herself loose. Janet looked around, "This is amazing! I'm sorry I haven't been here in so many years."

Hunter shrugged. Janet had changed. She was definitely an older woman now. She had gained weight. Her suit was stylish, but covered a few bulges he had never seen on her before.

"Thank you for coming to see the gallery. It's so good to see you," he said sincerely.

"Likewise, Hunter. Please show me around."

Hunter began the tour. "Here in the front area is the work of our *Artist of the Month*. Shelly Kellogg's work is post-modern as you can see." Hunter leaned close and whispered, "Personally I don't care for this style, but it's been selling."

"What I really came to see was you and your work," Janet replied.

"Right this way." Hunter led her farther back where they stopped in front of one of his newer favorites.

Janet burst out laughing. "That is so funny!" The sailor's hat was blowing away from the boat just beyond his reach. She stepped closer to take a better look. She glanced down at the title and price. "Hunter!" she scowled. "You change that price right now! That's worth twice that much!"

Hunter smiled and took a deep breath. "Oh Janet. You are such an encourager."

Janet smiled and continued her tour admiring painting after painting. "Do you remember last time I was here?" she asked.

"I sure do. You left a note and a very large check."

"My dad loves that painting. He thanks me and makes comments on it every time I visit."

"I'm glad he is still enjoying it."

When they reached the back of the gallery Hunter pointed at his desk. "This is where I do the business." He looked at Janet, "And this is where I should be doing more marketing."

Janet shook her head, "Oh Hunter, let's face it, you're a painter. Why, just look at all those canvases stacked behind the file cabinet."

"I know, I know. If you think this is bad, you should see my apartment."

"What's wrong with your apartment?"

"It's a mess. I've got paintings stacked against every wall."

"That sounds familiar," Janet shook her head. "And what about the knitting?" she smiled.

It was their secret. He hoped she had never told anyone. "Janet, no one knows but you. Well, Clara did, but she's gone. Look." Hunter leaned behind his desk and pulled open the bottom drawer.

Janet laughed and grabbed Hunter's arm as he slid the drawer shut. "Don't worry. I won't tell a soul! Never have. Never will." She pulled on Hunter's arm and gave him a hug.

The two of them strolled toward the front of the store. "Just a minute," Janet said, stopping in her tracks. She reached into her purse and pulled out her checkbook.

"What are you doing?" Hunter asked.

"Just writing a check," she replied. "I told you *The Sailor's Hat* was worth this much, so I'm adding a hundred for shipping."

"Janet, no. It's not worth THAT much," Hunter argued.

"As Clara used to say, Stop arguing." Janet ripped out the check and handed it to Hunter.

He looked at it in disbelief.

"I'll see you next time I'm in town." She reached out and hugged him again before moving out the door.

Hunter waved as she walked toward her car, then he turned away. He didn't want her to see him crying.

CHAPTER THIRTY-FIVE

THE CALL SHE WAS DREADING

Janet returned to California refreshed by her visit with her parents and with Hunter. Her folks were glad to hear Ralph was doing well, but they expressed disappointment at no longer being able to visit their grandchildren. Janet was thankful her parents were still in fairly good health. She was excited to receive *The Sailor's Hat*, her newest investment in Hunter Art. As she reflected on the visit, she was sad remembering Hunter's comment about his apartment. She pictured the paintings lining the room as they had so many years ago. There was no way she could help him from California. Besides, her new position as Regional Vice-President demanded her full attention.

Since the promotion her faithfulness at the gym had declined. She was self-conscious about her new outfits chosen to hide the weight she had gained. Church attendance was still important to her and only involved a once a week commitment. She was enjoying occasional visits with her neighbor Maria. This month she was celebrating another milestone.

"Hello, Maria. I'm calling with an invitation to you and the boys. I'm inviting all the neighbors to my home for an Open House on Saturday evening. Do you think you can come?"

"I'd be most happy to accept your invitation, señora. I don't think the boys will come. They feel awkward in a group of grown-ups."

"I understand, but they are certainly welcome."

Saturday evening Janet's little home was filled with neighbors. Her brother Ralph was there also. After everyone had arrived and helped themselves to drinks and snacks, Janet made her announcement.

"May I have your attention please?" Several guests clinked their glasses with a fork. "I appreciate you all coming to share this special occasion with me. I didn't tell anyone the reason for this Open House, but I am excited to announce that my mortgage was paid off this month and I am now a debt-free home owner."

The room erupted with applause. "Congratulations!" was shouted from several guests.

"I am so pleased to be a part of this neighborhood. Some of you welcomed me when I first came here to LA, and some of you came here after I did. I just wanted to share my joy and excitement with all of you." Another round of applause. "Please feel free to help yourselves to any of the snacks and drinks. Mí cása es sú cása. I learned that from Maria." Janet nodded a smile to Maria. The talking and laughter continued, much to Janet's delight.

With her mortgage paid, Janet opted to put an even larger percentage of her salary into the retirement annuity. It was already doing well, but now began growing rapidly. Janet had every reason to celebrate. In the months that followed, a sinking feeling returned to her stomach. She had so many reasons to be thankful, but the annoying voice in her kept asking, *So what?*

For several weeks she went to the gym every night after work. She was physically sore, but it seemed to be helping her depression. She pulled an old drawing from the drawer in the kitchen. Physical, mental, emotional, and spiritual. What was missing? Her body was healthy. Her mind was challenged at work every day. She worshiped weekly and prayed daily. What was wrong with her emotional life? Why did she feel adrift? Without purpose?

It was fall. It used to be her favorite season. The air in Chicago was crisp and filled her with energy. She loved the cooler nights, the anticipation of the holidays. Here in California there seemed to be no change of seasons. The days became shorter, but the smog and traffic persisted. The palm trees swayed as they had all summer. The buzz of an incoming phone call brought her back to the moment.

"Hi Janet. This is Hunter."

"Hi Hunter. Good to hear from you. What's new?"

"I'm calling from the hospital."

"Oh no, what happened?"

"I went to the doctor yesterday because I wasn't feeling well."

"Oh Hunter. I'm sorry to hear that."

"He checked me over and insisted I come to the hospital for some tests." Hunter paused.

I guess it's gone to my liver."

"Cancer?" Janet asked horrified.

"Yeah, I guess melanoma can spread from lymph glands to other places. I guess I've got it in the liver."

"How serious is that? Can it be treated?"

"I guess so. They're planning to start chemo and radiation."

"Both at the same time?"

"They said it's stage IV. I guess that's the worst."

"Hunter, don't give up. You know I'll be praying for you."

"Thanks Janet. There's one more thing I wanted to talk to you about."

"What's that?"

"You remember my friend Nathan?"

"I do. He's helped you quite a bit, hasn't he."

"Yeah he has. Nathan came to visit me today. I asked him if he knew a good lawyer. He said he knew a guy who helped him set up the foundation for his gallery and helps him with his income tax returns. Then I asked if the attorney could help me write a will."

"A will? Oh Hunter, you're not thinking about dying are you?"

"To be honest, Janet, I am. I've been thinking about how courageous Bob Gerber was when he had cancer. I guess I should have made a will before this, but now I see no reason to put it off. Anyway, what I wanted to tell you is I've made a decision. I'm going to leave the gallery and all my paintings to you."

"What? Hunter! Are you out of your mind?" Janet was in shock. "What about your parents? Or why not leave it all to Nathan? He's been your friend as long as I have."

"I've thought about all those possibilities. My parents are fine. They don't need the hassle. And my dad never wanted me to be an artist in the first place. As for Nathan, yeah, he's been a good friend. But I owe so much more to you."

"But I'm in California and have a super-demanding job. What would I do with your gallery?"

"Sell it, I guess. I won't be here to see what you decide. You're a good businesswoman. I'm sure you can sell it without even leaving California."

"That's not quite what I meant. I meant, it's your legacy. I'd want to honor that. I don't know how, but that's what I'd want to do."

"I know, Janet. And that's exactly why I want to leave it all to you."

Janet started crying. Hunter waited. "I don't know what to say, Hunter."

"That's okay. I just wanted you to know what was coming. You give it some thought. I'm not gonna die tonight!" Hunter said emphatically.

"Hunter Schlewitz, I can't stand you!" Janet replied, teasing.

"Oh, and one more thing." Hunter paused for dramatic effect. "You'll get my knitting too. Just don't tell anyone where it came from. It's probably worth millions!"

"Your knitting?" Both of them laughed to relieve the tension. Hunter promised to call again with updates on his condition. Janet thanked him and hung up. It was the phone call she had dreaded. She didn't expect the part about his will. Hunter, Hunter, Hunter.

CHAPTER THIRTY-SIX

HEATHER

The news from Hunter certainly didn't help her mood. Her times at the gym were slipping toward once a week, usually on Saturday. Most nights Janet worked until six or seven. When she left the office she just didn't have the energy to go to the gym, change clothes, work out, shower; and then go home and fix dinner. Most evenings she grabbed something to eat on the way home. As soon as she walked in the door she sat at the kitchen counter, ate, and crashed.

What worried Janet the most about the company was the decline in sales in the Western Region ever since her promotion. At leadership meetings, there seemed to be a lot of friction between the marketing team and the sales team now being led by her friend Heather. This morning's meeting was no exception.

"Janet, you know marketing," Heather began. "You know it shouldn't take more than a week or two to get a new sales campaign up and running."

"Well, Heather, that all depends on the nature of the campaign."

"Oh, come on. You've been briefed on our mid-year strategy. Why is it taking marketing so long to respond?"

"I'd like to answer that, Janet, if I may." It was Karl who responded. He had taken Janet's place as leader of the marketing team.

"Please, Karl," Janet replied.

"The issue is funding. It seems our CFO has some issues with the expenditures of the sales department. That's why we haven't been able to move forward with our plan."

"I can't believe it," Heather responded. "Now you're going to blame US?"

"Not exactly. I'm just explaining what's holding up the campaign," Karl replied.

"But the budget for this project was approved three months ago!" Heather responded.

"Okay, okay. Let me look into this," Janet interrupted. "I know Ed. He's been CFO as long as I can remember. I'll talk to him in Chicago and get this straightened out."

Janet sensed something about Heather. She remembered how competitive and driven Heather always was at the gym. She remembered how Heather had challenged her during workouts.

Janet recalled a conversation from the gym, how she had told Heather she just couldn't compete with her. "I admire your discipline, Heather, but I'll never be able to keep up with you. I think I'll just set my own pace and goals. I hope you don't mind."

"No, I don't mind," Heather had said. "I just thought you needed the incentive."

Now it seemed Heather was challenging her at work. They hadn't spoken to each other as friends for many months. At the office Heather was all business. But sales revenue was declining. Why? Maybe it wasn't anything within the company. Maybe it was industry wide. Maybe it was related to the national economy. But what really upset Janet was a nagging feeling that Heather was subtly undermining all of their efforts. Could she be intentionally trying to make me look bad? Or could she be jealous of me? Was she upset that I got the promotion to Regional Vice-President instead of her?

Retirement kept looking more and more appealing.

CHAPTER THIRTY-SEVEN

HUNTER'S BATTLE

I t was Hunter's second time in the hospital in less than a month. He was feeling rotten and hoped desperately the doctor could do something about it.

"Good morning, Hunter. I'd like to introduce you to a couple of team members who will be working together with me to beat this cancer."

"Good morning, Doc. I'm tired of feeling so shitty. What do you recommend?"

"This is Dr. Tsukamaki, he's in charge of radiation therapy, and this is Dr. Johnson who will oversee your chemo. Unfortunately, the cancer has affected your lymph nodes and liver which means we will have to be very aggressive in fighting it. Are you ready for the battle?"

"As ready as anyone can be, I guess."

"I'll be monitoring you very closely with blood tests as well as one more biopsy. But first I've written some prescriptions to help control your pain and the side effects of all these drugs. Do you have any questions?"

"No. I just want to feel better."

"The nurse will be in shortly to get your IV meds started, and you've already had the oral medications this morning. I think you'll notice a difference within twelve hours."

"I hope so. Thanks, Doc." Hunter watched the three white coats vanish like an apparition from his room.

If the pain medications did help that day, Hunter couldn't remember. All he knew was that the chemo was making him sicker. Or maybe it was the radiation. His nausea came in like the tide. At least twice a day, sometimes three or four times a day. Then there was peace, at least for his stomach, for a few hours. But his muscles ached from head to toe. The nurses brought warm blankets, compression socks for his sore calves, and pills, pills, and more pills. He couldn't sleep well at night because of the chills and fever.

Hunter wasn't sure how long he had been in the hospital, it seemed like forever. It was at the end of week two he had a better day. He woke up feeling nearly normal. His body ached, but so far, no nausea and no chills. Finally, he hoped the tide had turned. With his mind a little clearer, he wanted to talk to his parents, and Janet. She was probably at work so he called his parents first.

"Hi, Mom. How are you this morning?"

"Hello Hunter. I'm doing pretty good, just the usual aches and pains."

"Tell me about it." Hunter said sarcastically. "I've been having a few myself."

"I'm sorry your dad and I haven't been there to see you. I told you, Dad has a terrible cold and we wouldn't want to expose anyone at the hospital."

"Yeah, you told me. I guess at this point I could care less if I got a cold."

"Oh, honey, you sound kind of discouraged."

"You might say that. I feel like I've been through hell."

"How are the treatments going?"

"Yesterday I was going to tell the doctor to stop. I couldn't take any more. But today I'm feeling just a little better. So maybe they're starting to work, or my body is adjusting, or something. I'm totally wiped out."

"I hope you'll be feeling better soon. Dad and I love you, you know."

"Yeah, Mom, I know. I love you too."

"Well, you take care. And Dad and I will come see you as soon as he's feeling better."

"Okay, Mom, good bye." Hunter was relieved he had called. It was just good to hear his mom's voice.

Early that evening, remembering the time difference, he called Janet in California.

"Hi Janet, Hunter here."

"Hey, Hunter, you still in the hospital? I didn't recognize the number."

"Yeah, two weeks now. And I'm sick of it."

"How's it going?"

"The short answer is, Terrible. Today is the first day I've had any hope at all. Feeling just a little better. Yesterday I wanted to holler stop, but the doctor never came in. The nausea and pain and muscle aches have been unbearable. Oh, and the chills. I hate the chills and shaking. That comes and goes."

"Oh Hunter, I'm so sorry to hear this. Sounds miserable."

"It has been. I hope today is a turning point, otherwise, I quit. I just can't face another week like the ones I've been going through."

"That reminds me, do you remember what old Bob Gerber said?"

"Oh yeah, I remember I asked him why he didn't want any chemo. He said he'd rather die. You know, I understand now. I really do understand. I think I've reached that point."

"Please don't say that, Hunter. You're only in your forties, not eighty like Bob was."

"Sorry to correct you, Janet, but I turned fifty last year."

"Yeah, but you're still young. You've got a lot of good years left."

"I used to think so, but now I'm not so sure."

"I'm praying for you, Hunter. And God is with you. You'll get through this."

"Yeah, one way or another. Thanks for caring about me, Janet."

"Of course, and thanks for calling, Hunter. It's good to hear your voice."

That night, Hunter couldn't sleep. His chills returned. His muscles ached. And most embarrassing of all was the vomiting of bile all over his sheets and blanket at 3 a.m.

When the doctor came the next morning Hunter announced his decision. "No more."

"Are you sure?" the doctor asked.

"No more chemo, no more radiation. Please just give me something for pain and let me rest." Hunter replied.

The doctor didn't argue, didn't try to convince him to continue. The tests this week had shown the cancer was in other organs as well.

CHAPTER THIRTY-EIGHT

JANET DECIDES

The call came just before midnight. Janet recognized the number of the Chicago hospital. She had a feeling, a sinking, horrible feeling. If Hunter was okay, he wouldn't be calling this late.

"Hello, Ms. Sadler?"

"Yes, speaking."

"I'm calling about our patient, Hunter Schlewitz. His medical record indicated you were one of the persons he wished to notify." The nurse hesitated. "I'm very sorry to inform you that Hunter has just passed away."

"Thank you for calling. I've spoken with Hunter a couple of times this past week. I think he was ready for the end."

"We, at Chicago General, did all we could. He seemed to be resting well this evening. We did our best to keep him comfortable."

"Thank you for all the care you gave him. Have you talked to his parents?"

"Yes, I spoke with them just a few minutes ago."

Janet was numb. She thought she was prepared, but the reality of her friend's death took time to sink in. She kept waiting for him to call with another report. Then she would remember most vividly the call from the nurse. Hunter was gone.

A few days later she received a call from his parents. Charles and Helen were nervous about talking to Janet. They never quite understood the relationship between her and Hunter. At the very least they wanted Janet to know about plans for the memorial service, and whether or not she wanted to come.

"Have you set a date?" Janet asked.

"Not yet," Hunter's mother answered. "Hunter wished to be cremated, so there isn't any rush to have the memorial right away."

"I really would like to be a part of the service if that's at all possible. It would help if I had a week to wrap up some things here at my office."

"One of the dates we were looking at is the thirtieth, the last Saturday of this month," Hunter's dad suggested. "Would that work for you?"

Janet checked her calendar, "Yes, I could come then. Are you sure that works for you?"

"Definitely," Steve replied. "We'll work out the details. And we'll look forward to meeting you."

"Likewise. Hunter spoke highly of you both. I guess, since our relationship was strictly a business relationship, Hunter never felt it was important for us to meet."

"Yes, shortly before he died, Hunter explained that he was leaving the gallery and all his paintings to you. We know you meant a great deal to him," Helen spoke tenderly.

"We'll talk more about that at the end of the month. Until then, you two take care of each other. I'm sure it's hard losing your son. And I'll miss a dear old friend."

During the next two weeks Janet made plans for her trip to the Midwest. She had two weeks' vacation time available. Why not take some time with her parents? Or a week of relaxing and touring in Chicago? On the twenty-fifth she received a registered letter from a law firm in Chicago. It was a copy of Hunter's will and a copy of the lease for the gallery. As Hunter had promised she was the sole heir of his paintings. A signed document also turned over the ownership of Hunter Gallery to Janet Sadler.

During those weeks Janet also made a decision about her job. Next year she would turn sixty. Why not take early retirement? Why continue with all the stress and fatigue? Why not turn it all over to Heather since she seems to want it so much? Janet decided she would come back from Chicago and announce her retirement.

The confusion about funding which had caused such a stir at the office was finally resolved. The sales campaign was underway and the month of April was drawing to a close. Janet had shared the news of her friend Hunter's death with her closest colleagues. At the meeting on Monday, Janet announced to the entire staff that she was going to Chicago for a friend's memorial service. "I'll be leaving on Wednesday, and I'll be gone two weeks. If anything urgent arises, just call me," she said. She wished everyone well. After the meeting many co-workers, including Heather, came to express their sympathy and to wish her a good trip.

Janet's parents met her at O'Hare and brought her home to Milwaukee for a short visit before the service for Hunter. Janet called Steve and Helen Schlewitz to check on last minute details. She had agreed to do a brief eulogy and told them she was ready.

The memorial was held at the funeral home late Saturday morning. There were between twenty and thirty people in attendance, mostly friends of Hunter's parents. After the service several people introduced themselves as friends of Hunter, telling Janet they owned one or two of his paintings.

The only person Janet was really looking for was Nathan. She remembered how helpful he had been in Hunter's early years as an artist and gallery owner, and she wanted to reconnect. A heavy-set gentleman with a beard approached her. "Nathan?" she asked, as she struggled to recognize him.

Nathan opened his arms and gave her a big bear hug. "You did a nice job on Hunter's eulogy."

"Thank you, but I should have said more about you, and all you did for Hunter."

"Naa, today was for remembering Hunter," Nathan shrugged.

"I believe he told me you were friends in college?" Janet asked.

"Yeah, in fact we were in high school together. At the time we both wanted to be artists. Once I got into college I realized how hard it would be to make a living just doing art."

"I'm sure that's why many people only do art as a hobby."

"I gotta hand it to Hunter. He never gave up. He just kept painting." Nathan grinned.

"He was an artist to the core," agreed Janet. "And I remember many years ago when the only gallery in Chicago to display his paintings was yours."

"I always admired his work. And I was really excited for him when he got his own gallery."

"Hunter told me you helped him with some business ideas for his new gallery."

"Just a few suggestions. I really wanted him to succeed."

"So did I," Janet replied. "I just didn't know a thing about art."

"There's a rumor going around that Hunter left his art work and gallery to you."

"True. But I confess I don't know why." Janet shook her head.

"I know why. He respected you. He liked you. He appreciated all the help you gave him. And one more reason . . . he knew you would help his children, that's what he called his paintings, find a new home." Nathan smiled.

Janet smiled but felt her eyes welling with tears. "I hope we can talk again soon about his paintings and the gallery. Do you mind if I call you?"

"Not at all," Nathan replied. He pulled out his wallet. "Here's my business card. Call me any time. I'd love to hear from you."

That afternoon Janet joined the Schlewitz's at the cemetery for a committal of Hunter's ashes. It was there that Helen dug into her purse and handed Janet the keys to Hunter's Gallery and his apartment. Janet promised to bring Hunter's personal belongings back to them. They hugged good-bye and drove their separate ways. Janet drove to the gallery, memories swirling. She unlocked the door and went in. The front walls of the gallery were bare, waiting for the next guest artist. She wandered back to view Hunter's art. And she cried.

Janet stayed in the gallery less than an hour. She sat in Hunter's chair, glanced through the desk drawers, and found all of Hunter's business forms. She smiled when she opened the bottom drawer and found Hunter's knitting. She smiled, and then she cried again.

She left the door sign CLOSED, locked up, and headed for Milwaukee. It would be good to spend more time with her parents. There was a lot to talk about.

A week later Janet returned to Chicago. This time she went to the apartment. It was eerie walking into the lobby where she used to pull her mail from the box, many years ago. She grabbed the rail and climbed the stairs to the second floor. She stopped and looked at the final stair on which Hunter had tripped and spilled the groceries. The beginning of the Hunter Art Corporation meetings. Trembling with grief and nostalgia, she put the key into the lock and entered Hunter's apartment. They were there, just as Hunter had told her on the phone. His paintings lined the walls and floor of his living room. On the floor they were standing two and three deep. She stared at the paintings, her inheritance, a challenge, and her future. She knew it was the right decision. She would retire from the corporate world. She would return to Chicago. She would start a new chapter in her life. She would market Hunter's legacy. It seemed God had a hand in this, preparing her in so many ways for this new purpose. Janet felt a glimmer of excitement flickering in her heart. She had succeeded in business. She was confident she would succeed again. It was time to get to work.

Janet had three days before her return flight to California. Three days to get this apartment cleaned out and locked up. The first and most obvious to her were the paintings. She began loading them into her car and taking them to the gallery. She made two trips before dinner, took a break to eat, and made two more trips that evening. She checked into a hotel room, showered, and hit the bed.

The next morning she tackled the bedroom. She sorted what could be thrown out, what could be given to Goodwill, and what should be taken to Hunter's parents. Next was the kitchen. A few items for his parents, the rest to Goodwill. Load the car. Take things to their destination. She had a brief visit with Charles and Helen who shed a few tears when Janet gave them Hunter's clothes and personal belongings. A second night at the hotel. One day to go.

Day three. Janet stood staring at Hunter's easels, acrylics, palettes, sketch books, and brushes. There were small boxes full of pencils, erasers, palette knives, exacto blades, and other items she couldn't name. She carried the easels and slid them into the back of her car. Next, a couple of large cardboard boxes for transporting all the odds and ends of the artist. She loaded those into her car and drove everything to the gallery. She would deal with all of it when she returned from California. She called the apartment manager to report the apartment was empty, though it did need a thorough cleaning. She was instructed to return the key by mail.

CHAPTER THIRTY-NINE

LOOSE ENDS

It felt strange flying to California for perhaps the last time. She would have to see her brother and share her decision with him. Would he consider returning to the Midwest? Will he get married again someday? The clouds moved by below her. How would her decision be received at the office? At corporate in Chicago? How would she handle the selling of her home in South Park? What would she want to take back to Chicago? Where should she live when she moved back to Illinois? Her thoughts were interrupted by a whirring noise and a sudden thump. The landing gear. In moments the plane was on the ground at LAX.

The following week Janet made her announcement, early retirement beginning June 1. The office staff congratulated her and thanked her for her contributions. Karl's handshake and compliments felt genuine, Heather's did not.

"Congratulations, Janet, it's been such a pleasure working with you."

"Thank you, Heather," Janet replied.

JIM BORNZIN

"You've challenged us in so many ways! I don't know what we'll do without you."

It was just too much. Janet smiled and continued greeting others in the office.

At home Janet began packing up the things she would ship to Chicago, and things she would take in her car. She contacted a realtor and made arrangements to sell the house. The rising market in L.A. housing meant a good profit for Janet, and of course, a nice commission for the realtor.

Janet was excited about one other idea. She issued another invitation to her home for an Open House on Saturday, May 23. Please come for an outdoor barbeque pot-luck dinner and games.

That afternoon the grill was lit and the hamburgers ready. Beach balls, balloons, and a treasure hunt were prepared. One neighbor agreed to bring his grill and prepare hot dogs. Maria brought mountains of chimichangas. Fred and Barbara brought a large tub full of ice and beer. After everyone had eaten Janet made her announcement.

"At our last open house, I announced that I was the proud owner of this lovely home. It seemed only right to invite all of you to share my newest joy. I have decided to sell this lovely place to someone new so that I can return to my home in Illinois."

It was a mixed message. Neighbors were not sure if they should cheer or cry. There was an awkward silence as everyone tried to decide what to say. Finally someone said, "We'll miss you." Others joined the chorus, "We're gonna miss you Janet."

Fred raised his can of beer and hollered, "Here's to good neighbors!" Others shouted, "To good neighbors!" and "To Janet!" Small groups began discussing the announcement.

Maria made her way closer to Janet. "I am very sad, amíga. Why are you leaving us?"

"I have decided to take early retirement. The work I've been doing is very stressful. When I go back to Chicago, I will own a small art gallery. I will also live much closer to my parents who are becoming quite elderly."

"I understand. But I will miss you very much," Maria opened her arms for a hug.

The realtor called the day before Janet left. She had a buyer who was very interested. Financing needed to be arranged. She would fax the papers for the closing to Chicago. Janet thanked her and finished loading the car. Everything had gone well. She was on her way home.

CHAPTER FORTY

A NEW CHAPTER BEGINS

J anet took four days to drive back to Chicago. She had seen the
Grand Canyon many years ago as a young adult and had always
dreamed of returning. That was her first destination. The second
day she drove to Vail, Colorado. She had never been there before.
She rode a gondola up the mountainside, then strolled the shops and
stores that evening. The third day was devoted to a leisurely drive
to Des Moines, Iowa. The cornfields reminded her that she was
back in the Midwest. The fourth day she arrived in Chicago. She
had made a reservation at The Robey, a romantic hotel on North
Division, only a mile from the Hunter Gallery. Ah, it was good to
be back!

Her first concern was to find a house or apartment, not too
far from the gallery. She spent two days checking the real estate
ads and visiting as many places as she could. The apartment she
found was on Division, just a little farther west than the gallery. It
was spacious and newly remodeled, and she loved it! Janet signed

the lease, unloaded the car, and started sending everyone her new address.

She called Nathan and he agreed to meet her at Hunter's gallery the next day. When he arrived Janet was busy at the desk trying desperately to access the records on Hunter's laptop. Janet rose to welcome Nathan and explained what she was trying to do. "Do you have any idea what Hunter might have used for a password?" Janet asked.

"I have no idea. Have you looked through the desk drawers?" Nathan replied.

"See, I knew there was a reason I invited you here this morning," Janet teased as she began rifling through the top drawer. "Ha! Look at this." Janet pulled a scribble pad from the desk with several notes that looked like they might be passwords or PINs. "You're a genius." She smiled at Nathan.

In a short time they figured out how to access Hunter's records for sales and inventory. Janet asked Nathan if Hunter had expressed any other desires for his paintings or for the gallery.

"Not that I can recall," Nathan replied. "He was very clear that he wanted you in charge of everything."

"Well I've been thinking. I would like to bequeath to you, on Hunter's behalf, any painting of your choice. I feel certain Hunter would approve."

"Are you sure?" Nathan was taken aback.

"Absolutely. Do you have one in mind?"

"No. I've never thought about it. May I have some time to decide? Or do you want me to choose one today?"

"There's no hurry. But as long as you're here, I would appreciate a hand pulling out the paintings from behind the file cabinet. I'd like to make sure they are all have titles, and are recorded as inventory. Then we'll go through all the paintings I brought from Hunter's apartment. Do you have time to help me with that?"

"Sure," Nathan answered. "Today was for helping Janet. And if we go through all the paintings, maybe I'll find one I might like to own."

"It's a win-win for both of us," Janet smiled.

They managed to review nearly a hundred and twenty of Hunter's works. There were eight pieces without titles and uncatalogued in the laptop. Janet copied Hunter's records onto a flash drive before locking up for the night. And Nathan left with a painting from the Chicago period.

The next few days Janet spent updating the website and reviewing Hunter's social media. She used those platforms to introduce herself as the new owner and manager of the Hunter Gallery.

She began planning for a new "opening" which she could publicize. It would be dedicated to Hunter's memory, and be devoted to Hunter's best works. Janet was truly excited.

A week after moving into her new apartment, Janet received a hand-written letter from Maria. She tore it open and began reading.

Dear Janet,

> *I miss you very much. I think of you every time I make chimichangas. The new owners moved into your house a couple of days ago, but I haven't met them yet. Maybe I will take them a bag of chimichangas like I did for you.*
>
> *I want to thank you for the help and encouragement you gave my son Ricardo. This past Saturday was his graduation from Cal Tech. It never would have been possible without the gift of five thousand dollars you gave him to go to college.*
>
> *I hope you are doing well at the art gallery and in your new home.*

Your friend,
Maria

Janet had almost forgotten the gift she had given to Ricardo when he graduated from high school. She pressed Maria's letter against her heart. Who needed who? Maria had certainly been a good neighbor, and had not been afraid to reach across cultural boundaries. God bless her.

Janet was so excited about the Re-Opening Night at Hunter Gallery. The website and advertising all announced new hours, Tuesday – Thursday and Sunday noon to 6 pm. Friday and Saturday noon to 8 pm. Janet wanted morning hours for herself to fix up the apartment and do her shopping. She wanted Sunday morning for church attendance. She added a feminine touch to the gallery with flower arrangements on the window ledges and on several pedestals. She put a 6' screen wall in front of the desk and file cabinet and bought a new computer and printer for the office.

The visitors began on Friday afternoon, slowly at first. But after working hours, the rush hour began. The table with appetizers and wine was so crowded visitors had to wiggle their way forward to reach the snacks. Small groups gathered in front of the featured paintings talking about why they liked it and what they saw in each work. Janet was thankful for Nathan's presence. He had agreed to write up any sales so Janet could mingle with the visitors. Between 6 and 8 pm there was hardly room to move inside the gallery, and it became quite warm with all the bodies inside. Several people stood in line at the small office wall waiting their turn to make a purchase.

When the evening ended, Janet bid the last visitors good-bye, turned out the lights and locked the door. She was smiling gratefully as she moved back toward the office area. "How did we do?" she asked Nathan.

"You won't believe it," he replied. "Fourteen paintings sold, for a total of $56,800."

"Amazing!" Janet replied. "Thank you so much for your help."

"My pleasure," Nathan said as he rose from the office chair. "It's the least I could do, for my old buddy Hunter, and for you."

Janet's new chapter in Chicago had brought new purpose to her new life.

CHAPTER FORTY-ONE

BALANCE RESTORED

S uccessful marketing had always been Janet's talent. Now she had a product she could market with a personal enthusiasm she never had before. Hunter's paintings were all masterpieces of varying size and degrees. The first several months at the gallery were spent getting to know customers, other gallery owners, and the artists who had been featured in past years. She realized she didn't have to know a lot about art; she just had to enjoy people. It was a whirlwind and Janet was loving it.

Getting settled in her new apartment was also fun and challenging. She had given her cat and most of her plants to Maria before leaving L.A. She purchased new furniture, hung Hunter's art work, and organized her kitchen and bedroom closet. The first month had flown and she still had not gotten acquainted with others in the building. She promised herself she would. It was just before noon when her phone rang. The number was the corporate office in L.A.

"Hello, this is Janet."

"Good morning, Janet, this is Karl."

"Oh hi Karl, so good to hear your voice. How are things at the office?"

"I thought you'd be interested in an update. First the good news, I got a promotion."

"Congratulations! Salary increase or new title too?" Janet could hardly wait.

"Western Region, Vice-President. I'm going to have to try and fill your old shoes."

"Good luck, buddy. It's a lot of responsibility, that's for sure. But I'm really happy for you. Did you have something else to report?"

"Well, the not-so-good news is that your old friend Heather has resigned."

"Heather resigned? I can't believe it."

"The rumor from the sales section is she thought she would get V.P. Apparently she was very upset she didn't get it."

"Hmm, to be honest, I guess that doesn't surprise me. She was always very competitive."

"Heather was a hard worker, and I hated to see her go."

"Maybe there will be less competition between departments now," Janet suggested.

"That might be, but now I have the responsibility of finding her replacement."

"That's why they're paying you the big bucks, Karl," Janet giggled.

None of what he told her came as a surprise. Karl had been so easy to work with as part of the marketing team. She was glad he had been promoted. And Heather? Heather was tough. She'd find a good position in some other company. Maybe with the competition. Ha!

Janet tried worship at two of the Lutheran churches in the neighborhood. Both appeared to be struggling to pay the pastor with a dwindling membership and few young people. She wanted to believe she was younger than the gray hairs she saw in church, but the truth was in the mirror each morning. One of the congregations was extremely welcoming and the pastor put Janet at ease with her spontaneous outpouring of laughter. This was the community she would now call "home."

She found a nearby fitness club which seemed clean and friendly. They had a reduced membership rate for seniors over sixty. Janet laughed. She'd just wait two more months and get the cheaper membership.

Tuesday noon, the beginning of her "work week." She almost laughed as she walked along Division toward the gallery. The sun was shining and it hadn't rained for weeks. She was in Chicago, in an apartment, and working in an art gallery. It was like a dream. She glanced up at the sign above the door and said a little prayer, *Thank you Hunter Schlewitz*.

The bell jingled as she entered, bringing a smile to her face. She turned the sign to OPEN and looked around the gallery. It was hers. The phone on the desk started ringing so she ran to answer it.

"What time do you open?" the caller wanted to know.

"Noon to six today through Thursday, noon to eight on Friday and Saturday."

"Thank you," the caller said and hung up.

She turned on the computer and began responding on social media. An hour later the bell rang announcing visitors to the gallery. Janet rose and went to meet them. It was an elderly couple from the neighborhood.

"Welcome to the Hunter Gallery. My name is Janet and I'm the new manager."

"How do you do? We're the Johnson's and we live in the apartment building across the street."

"Have you been here before?" Janet asked.

"Oh my, yes. Quite often. We like to come in and browse around when we're out walking."

"Walking is a wonderful exercise, especially when the weather is as nice as it is today." Janet couldn't help but think about the Gerbers.

"We even bought one of Hunter's paintings a few years ago," Mr. Johnson smiled at his wife.

"Do you mind if I ask which one?" Janet replied.

"It's a lovely fall scene," Mrs. Johnson answered. "It has lots of trees, bright yellow and orange leaves, and long, dark shadows because the sun is setting. I think Hunter told us he painted it at one of the forest preserves."

"Then that would be from his Chicago period about ten years ago. It was a very prolific time for him."

"Oh, did you know Hunter too?" Mrs. Johnson asked excitedly.

"Yes. I certainly did. We were very good friends." Janet smiled.

"We were so glad the gallery re-opened," Mr. Johnson added.

"I was happy to do it," Janet smiled again.

"Well, you take care now. We'll see you next time we're out." Mr. Johnson waved his hand as he and his wife turned to leave.

What a lovely couple, Janet thought to herself.

Janet's second month featured a new young artist, only 22, who had never shown work in a gallery before. He promised to sit at the gallery each Sunday from noon until 6. That gave Janet a chance to drive up to Milwaukee to see her folks after church on Sunday. Sometimes she stayed a couple of days and then drove back to Chicago in time to open the gallery at noon on Tuesday.

With a growing social media following and a website updated weekly, gallery attendance remained strong. Janet was thrilled whenever she was able to sell a piece to someone from out-of-town or across the country. It began with a social media inquiry or an email, and ended with her shipping the artwork UPS or Fed Ex. Her life was in balance, and she couldn't be happier.

CHAPTER FORTY-TWO

SHE GIVES THEM WINGS

The Johnsons returned to the gallery a week later. Janet greeted them warmly. "Hi folks! You out for your exercise again?"

"Well, yes we are, but that's not the main reason we came in," Mrs. Johnson declared.

Mr. Johnson continued, "We saw a painting last week that we hadn't see before and we wanted to look at it again."

"Was it hanging on one of the gallery walls?" Janet asked.

"Right over there," Mrs. Johnson pointed across the room.

The three of them walked to the painting and stood there staring. There was a bright blue sky above Lake Michigan, two sailboats, one in the foreground and one in the distance. Beyond the distant sailboat dark thunderclouds were building up over the lake. A flash of lightening dropped from the black cloud to the lake surface just beyond the second boat.

"That's a very dramatic scene," Janet finally commented.

"With the whitecaps and the sailboat heeling to port, I can almost feel the wind," Mr. Johnson exclaimed.

"And the lightening in the distance is very ominous," his wife added.

"I don't have my glasses on," Mr. Johnson declared, "how much are you asking for it?"

Janet glanced at the card below the painting, *Storm Brewing* is $850."

Mr. Johnson looked at his wife and tipped his head in question. She nodded yes, looked at Janet and smiled.

"Looks like you two will have another Hunter to enjoy."

As they sat at the desk writing a check Mrs. Johnson began to share a little about their family.

"Mr. Johnson and I are getting older and starting to think about the future. We won't be here forever you know. Well, we have a daughter and a son. One lives in Evanston and the other in Denver. We certainly don't want them fighting over the Hunter."

Mr. Johnson handed the check to Janet. "So we decided to purchase another Hunter."

"So when we're gone they'll each get one," Mrs. Johnson added.

"And hopefully not fight over the same one!" Mr. Johnson laughed.

Later that afternoon Janet was reflecting on the sale, and on the couple who seemed so pleasant. *When I was working I got along pretty well with my co-workers. Many became friends. But it's different now. Now it seems I'm just enjoying people for who they are, not for what they do. And I'm not trying so hard to please everyone, just enjoy them.*

As the months passed, more and more of Hunter's paintings left the gallery. There were less than a hundred remaining, of the original one hundred forty she had inherited. She almost hated to see them go. With each sale it felt like Hunter himself was slowly slipping from her life.

Her email exchanges with the Hunter Squared Gallery in Santa Fe, New Mexico, led to a pleasant business bond between the two "Hunter" galleries. The most recent email mentioned her latest posting on the website. They were interested in the featured painting of the *Chicago Skyline* as seen from the Navy Pier ferris wheel. Janet considered it impressionist style, perhaps more fitting for the Santa Fe gallery. The original asking price was $3000, but Janet agreed to sell for $2800 plus shipping costs. Another Hunter, gone.

During her second summer as gallery owner, Janet noticed a drop in visitors and sales. The burst of excitement with the re-opening and increased social media traffic was fading. She found herself spending more time in the chair near the window. She enjoyed watching people walk by, waving at those who were daily strollers. She was also enjoying books checked out from the local library. She remembered how Hunter had described Clara sitting in this very spot reading, and Hunter himself after Clara died. She vowed to herself, however, that she would never take up knitting!

Never before had Janet known such peace. Her ties with the corporate world were fading as well. Half a dozen Christmas cards had been received from former colleagues. Her friend Heather didn't send one and Janet had no idea where Heather now lived. There was also a phone call from Karl. Things were going well at the office, another good year for sales, just below Janet's record year before leaving. He wished her a blessed holiday.

How many more years would it take to sell all of Hunter's work? Three? Five? Time would tell. For now, it was the least stressful, most fulfilling time of her life. Her dad's health was failing. She was thankful to be living less than two hours from their home in Milwaukee. *If anything happens to Dad, Mom will need a lot of support.*

Sitting at the gallery window one day she was staring absently at the building across the street. She watched two young pigeons being pushed from the nest by their mother. Each one fluttered clumsily, nearly falling to the ledge above the storefront across from the gallery. Janet chuckled as the mother pigeon joined them on the ledge as if to say, "Good job! I knew you could do it!"

Janet began to cry. Those were the words she always wanted to say to Hunter. As hard as it was to like him, she had always loved his paintings. They were his children. He had given them birth. Now they were her children, all grown and ready to leave the nest. As each of Hunter's children left the gallery, she was as proud as a foster mom can be, that she had given them wings. They were taking on new life in a world of their own. Hunter would be pleased.

ABOUT THE AUTHOR

Jim Bornzin is a retired Lutheran pastor living in Silverton, Oregon. During fifty years of ordained ministry, he has served six congregations in Oregon, Washington, and Illinois. Jim also served as a hospital chaplain in Silverton, and a volunteer police chaplain in Coos Bay, Oregon.

He has worked with numerous community agencies: Habitat for Humanity, Helpline Information & Referral, and Temporary Help in Emergency House.

His first novel, *Terror at Trinity*, is available from iUniverse and Amazon. Jim also enjoys scissor-cutting, cabinet work, and writing poetic sermons. Please visit the author's website: **jimbornzin.com** to view his artwork, poetry, and sermons.

Blessed Are the Hungry is a heart-warming study of characters and their relationships. Despite their differences these four quirky characters utilize humor, patience, and wisdom to help each other. In the process they end uphelping themselves to find hope, purpose, and love. A fun and easy read.

Printed in the United States
By Bookmasters